D0840906

SUMMER AT CARRICK PARK

When Joel Leicester walks into the hotel where Rosa Tempest works, she can't believe her bad luck. The last time Rosa saw the man who broke her heart, it was after a holiday when they'd been greeted at his flat by a woman claiming to be his fiancée. Rosa never stuck around to hear Joel's side of the story. But now, six years on, fate has another trick up its sleeve as a potentially disastrous summer wedding at Carrick Park can only be saved by the two of them . . .

Books by Kirsty Ferry
in the Linford Romance Library:

EVERY WITCH WAY

KIRSTY FERRY

SUMMER AT CARRICK PARK

Complete and Unabridged

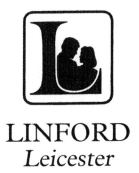

LINFORD
Leicester

First published in Great Britain in 2018 by
Choc Lit Limited
Surrey

First Linford Edition
published 2019
by arrangement with
Choc Lit Limited
Surrey

A catalogue record for this book is available
from the British Library.

ISBN 978–1–4448–4096–4

Published by
F. A. Thorpe (Publishing)
Anstey, Leicestershire

Set by Words & Graphics Ltd.
Anstey, Leicestershire
Printed and bound in Great Britain by
T. J. International Ltd., Padstow, Cornwall

This book is printed on acid-free paper

Dedication

For my grandma, Jennie Armstrong, whose scones were always flat but always delicious.

Acknowledgements

It's very dangerous to let me loose on a book that's largely based on cake, but it has happened. And I don't regret eating lots of cake in the name of research whilst writing this little story at all. However, a purely contemporary novella is a new departure for me, and I do hope that you enjoy reading it as much as I've enjoyed creating it.

Carrick Park is the hotel from my first Choc Lit book, *Some Veil Did Fall*, and also appears in my Christmas novella, *A Little Bit of Christmas Magic*. I thought such a lovely place deserved another story beyond the 'Rossetti Mysteries' series, and you might also recognise Rosa, Tara and Ailsa from previous books too. You might also recognise the little mention of Hartsford Hall from *Watch for me by Moonlight* and the wider 'Hartsford Mysteries' series.

Summer at Carrick Park, however, is, more than anything, Rosa Tempest's story. A couple of years ago, I read about a Lord Darcy who was part of the Pilgrimage of Grace against Henry VIII. His first wife was called Dousabella Tempest, and I thought it was such a fantastic name, I had to use it in some way. I didn't run with Dousabella, more's the pity, perhaps, but that is how I picked Tempest for Rosa, Jessie and Angel's surname. I therefore hope you enjoy this book and are happy to come back to hear more about 'my' Tempest sisters.

I must thank, as always, the Choc Lit team, without whom this wouldn't have happened. Thank you also to my wonderful editor and fabulous cover designer, and the truly awesome Choc Lit family — you are such a great group of people, and I know that we support each other tirelessly. I couldn't ask to be part of a better virtual family. Thanks also to the Tasting Panel who passed *Summer at Carrick Park* for publication: Janine N, Bianca B, Melissa B, Janet S, Sigi, Susan D, Katie P, Isabella T, Joy S, Alma H, Joanne B, Melissa E, Isabelle D, Isabel J, Dimi E, Claire W and Caroline U.

And last but definitely not least, I have to thank my lovely friends and my own family too — my parents, my husband, my son and my dog. Thank you for the wine and the chocolate and the coffee and the hugs.

And thank you very much for the cake — always the cake. Thank you!

The Bride-Cake

This day, my Julia, thou must make

For Mistress Bride the wedding-cake:

Knead but the dough, and it will be

To paste of almonds turn'd by thee;

Or kiss it thou but once or twice,

And for the bride-cake there'll
be spice.

Robert Herrick

1

Present Day

Rosa Tempest could often despair. Being the oldest of three sisters was sometimes extremely rewarding; but at other times, like today, it could be maddening.

She had already fielded a breathy call from her youngest sister, Angel, who was asking if she could let her know if there were any rooms free at her hotel for a particular date in August, in two weeks or so. 'Her' hotel, as Rosa stiffly told Angel, was usually fully booked for weddings around that time, but depending on what she wanted, she might be lucky. She would certainly check when she got to work to see if there was anything available. Rosa didn't own Carrick Park Hotel and was merely the senior receptionist, so she didn't know for sure off the top of her head whether there were any rooms free or not.

'Well can you at least *try* to find out pretty quickly and ring me back because Kyle needs to know because *family*.'

''Because family' what?' Rosa had asked, as she pushed her feet into her neat, navy-blue stilettoes.

'Because Kyle's family. His parents are coming over. They've never seen Taigh Fallon, and they're coming over from Canada; and after they've been to Scotland, they're coming back with us and staying in Yorkshire for a few days. Goth Cottage is too small. We've only got the one bedroom.'

Kyle had relocated from Ontario last year and now he and Angel split their time between Kyle's inherited Scottish house, Taigh Fallon, and Angel's tiny cottage in Whitby. Carrick Park was on the moors, a few miles away from Whitby, and would, Rosa knew, be perfect for Kyle's family to stay in.

Rosa was in the fortunate position that she had her own little cottage out on the moors — well, a small terraced house in a village out on the moors — which was, Angel said, as 'buttoned-up' as Rosa was. She also had the use of a room in the staff quarters at the hotel. There was no need for Angel to know that Rosa was working strange shifts that week and was taking advantage of the staff quarters, so she could find out room availability quite easily and quite quickly, and Rosa didn't enlighten her.

Instead, she had sighed and picked up a pen.

She pulled a hotel-issue notepad towards her and asked 'Is it just the one room you need? Give me some more details.'

Angel told her and Rosa fended off the thanks, and she had managed — eventually — to hang up on her sister and finish putting her make-up on.

She slung her bag over her shoulder and had one hand on the door handle when her phone rang again. Jessie. Her middle sister.

'Jessie. How lovely to hear from you,' Rosa said, flatly. 'What do you want? I'm just on my way to work — so make it quick.' There was no need for Jessie to know either, quite how close to work she actually was.

'Rosa — I'm after some advice.' There was a howl from somewhere in Suffolk, where Jessie now lived, and her sister sounded fraught. 'Wasp stings. Is it bicarbonate of soda or vinegar?'

The howl continued, gaining decibels and Rosa closed her eyes. At eight weeks old, Rosa's baby niece, Lottie, had a very good pair of lungs.

'Vasp — vinegar. Bee — bicarb. You *know* these things,' Rosa said.

'I knew them nine weeks ago,' wailed Jessie, 'but I don't know anything *now*.'

'Put vinegar on Lottie. But don't let Elijah mistake her for a chip.'

'It's Elijah that got stung!' cried Jessie, referring to her ten-year-old stepson. 'Lottie's just *shouting*.'

4

'Then put vinegar on *Elijah*!' said Rosa, exasperated. 'Look, I'm going to be late for work. I want to miss the traffic.'

'Okay, okay. I forget there's a world outside of nappies sometimes. Thank you.'

'Thank you, Rosa!' came a smaller, masculine voice from the background, thin and wavery above the crying Lottie; Elijah, sounding brave and pained at the same time. 'It was a really big wasp. It was vicious.'

Rosa couldn't help but smile. She had a lot of time for Elijah, despite the fact he was untidy and never seemed to shut up.

'Tell Elijah wasps are rarely cute and cuddly. Give me a bee any day,' said Rosa. 'Now, I've got to go. Hope the vinegar works for you.'

'Me too,' replied Jessie. 'Love you, Rosa.'

'Love you too.' Rosa hung up, thrust the phone in her bag and checked her reflection as she prepared to leave the room again. Not a blonde hair out of place, not a smudge of mascara anywhere. *Good.* She prided herself on good impressions and it was certainly an essential part of her job. Her younger sisters were much more lax — Angel dressed in black Victoriana, constantly, and Jessie was never happier than when she was in jeans and an anorak. Rosa had always had the reputation as the sensible one — and it was clear if anyone ever saw the three women together why.

Rosa did resent Angel's idea that she was 'buttoned-up' though. She leaned forward and dabbed at the corner of her lipstick, then pouted at herself in the mirror. She allowed herself a quick smile. She was probably on the wrong side of thirty to consider pouting — God, she was nearer to forty, when she thought about it — but it was comical. Then she stood up and sighed. She tugged her pencil skirt straight and hitched her shoulder bag up again, then left the room. Time to start a graveyard shift of sorts — 5 p.m. until 1 a.m. Thank God she had the bedroom at the hotel to collapse into afterwards.

★ ★ ★

Rosa clip-clopped along the corridor and down the service staircase that led around to the reception desk. Tiny, half-rusted bells hung high up along the corridor, but she had no time to drift past them and imagine the lives of the people who had rung them when Carrick Park Hotel was simply Carrick Park, home of the great Carrick family of Yorkshire.

Angel would have stood and stared, and sighed over the history of the place; Jessie would have idly wondered which one belonged to the library, then tracked her way to that room and rearranged half the books; but Rosa saw them almost every day and had more or less ceased noticing them. They were quaint pieces of decoration, and that was it.

'Good evening, Tara,' said Rosa as the mahogany-haired receptionist looked up at her and smiled. 'Have we been busy?'

Tara shook her head and her hair swung from side to side. 'Not too bad. There was a problem with someone's room service, in that they didn't get it. But it's fine now and they're happy enough.'

Rosa nodded. 'Good. I prefer starting a shift with nobody coming out shouting.' She smiled and waited until Tara had logged off the computer and vacated the desk.

'Have fun,' said Tara. She flashed a look at the clock and then looked at Rosa, and smiled sympathetically. 'I hate this shift. I feel sorry for you.'

'It's not as bad as one until nine. That shift is awful.' Rosa shuddered.

'It's a lot quieter, that one,' replied Tara. 'It's nice to have some down time. And it's even nicer if you've brought cake in.'

Tara looked at Rosa hopefully, but

Rosa shook her head. 'Not today. I need to buy some more flour. That one I made last week took everything I had out of the cupboard.' She referred to a five-layer, water-iced citrus cake that was mouth-wateringly divine, if she did say so herself. It hadn't even lasted an hour in the hotel; everyone had kept taking sly slices behind the scenes. 'Anyway, I don't mind finishing at one. Especially with having the bed upstairs. It's not too bad.'

'I suppose we don't have to drive home,' said Tara with a grin. 'I'll see you tomorrow. And buy more flour. Soon!'

'It's on my list,' confirmed Rosa. She slid into the seat and typed her details in, her fingernails perfectly French-manicured. She logged into the bookings system, and scrolled through until she found the dates Angel had asked her about. It was fortunate that there were a couple of rooms free and she booked one of them provision-ally for the Canadians. It was just as well they hadn't wanted to come the weekend before that — Ailsa, the Carrick Park Wedding Events Coordinator, had blocked out so many rooms for a wedding that the place was full, just as she had suspected. She smiled to herself. She knew how the place worked and it didn't prove much, but a small part of her felt smug.

She closed the system down. She'd give it a little while before she rang Angel. No need for her to realise that she'd done the job so quickly and efficiently: let her wait a bit. It wouldn't do her any harm.

2

'You've got it all sorted, yeah?' Luke sat back on the sofa and placed his feet on Joel's coffee table.

'By sorted you mean ... ?' Joel prompted Luke for an answer.

Luke apparently thought a shrug was enough of an answer; then, seeing Joel's eyes narrow dangerously, he seemingly decided to expand on it. 'The — ' he flapped his hand, lazily. 'The cars. The ring. The cake. The — *stuff.*'

'The stuff for *your* wedding?' Joel asked. 'The stuff you and Erica should have sorted. For God's sake — it's next week.'

'You're best *man,*' said Luke in that irritating, laid back drawl he had. 'You do all that, yeah?'

'No.' Joel lifted his friend's feet and shifted them roughly, dropping them back onto the floor. He pulled the table

11

away a metre or so, just to make sure he didn't try it again. 'I organised the stag do, I carry the rings on the day. I make sure you get your backside out of bed Saturday morning and get you to the ceremony on time.'

'Will Erica do it all then?' Luke asked. Joel couldn't believe how much his friend was annoying him.

'Are you genuinely stupid or just a good actor?' Joel asked. 'I think you and Erica need to kind of have a conversation?'

Luke nodded and yawned.

He stretched and then put his hands behind his head. 'A conversation. Yeah.'

'Unbelievable,' muttered Joel. He shook his head and asked in a louder voice, 'Do you actually *want* to get married?'

Luke stared at him. 'Well yes. I do.'

'So take an interest in it. Ask Erica if she needs any help.'

'Nah. Between Bridezilla and her Mumzilla, it's horrific.' He pulled a face. 'Spreadsheets. Shed loads of spreadsheets. Control freaks.'

'Then all that *stuff* will be sorted. You have no worries. Idiot.'

'I suppose.' Luke perked up. 'It'll be over with soon enough then we can go on the honeymoon.'

'You have sorted that, haven't you?' asked Joel, dreading the answer.

'Erica has. I said to just tell me where and when.' Luke smiled that lazy, lopsided smile that had had women swooning over him for as long as Joel had known him and stretched again. 'I think it's Paris. Or maybe Amsterdam. She might have said Venice.'

Joel stared at his friend disbelievingly. *Seriously?* He didn't even know where he was going on honeymoon?

Luke cast a glance at him askance, then grinned. 'Just joking. We're going to London for a couple of days then flying to Amsterdam. You know what Erica's like with her museums and her paintings. You've got Van Gogh over there and all the galleries in London. You know I'd do anything to keep her happy. God love her, she's worked hard enough to plan it all.' He stood up. 'I'd best get back. Erica said something about a dress fitting. I don't know if it's hers or hers and Bron's, but she said I had to be back to take the dog out before she went.' He pulled a face. 'It's not going to harm Murphy if I'm a bit late, though, is it?'

'It won't harm Murphy,' replied Joel, 'but Erica might harm you. Best get back, mate.'

Luke nodded. 'Yeah. Okay — so you're all sorted with your stuff?'

'I am.' Joel ushered him out. God, he loved Luke like a brother; but sometimes he just wanted to punch him. The man was so laidback he was almost horizontal.

'Oh!' Luke paused, in the doorway. 'Have you met Bron? Her Welsh friend.'

'Don't think so. Come on. Out. I've got stuff to do.'

'You'd like her.' Luke winked. 'I mean, *really* like her.'

Joel couldn't help but feel that old

block of ice reform in the pit of his stomach. 'No thanks.' He switched on a grin. 'Last time I really liked someone it didn't end well.'

'Yeah. Maybe if you don't cheat on the next one, it would end better.'

Joel opened his mouth to respond. Then he closed it again. The man was right. It was pointless entering into a debate about that one. He knew the truth and Luke did too, and Joel didn't find it very amusing, really.

'Ah — I knew there was something else!' Luke stopped again.

'Move! Leave!' growled Joel. 'Please, for the love of God! Go home. I'm not having Erica's expectations on my conscience.'

'No, no. Not her expectations — but!' Luke turned and grinned at Joel. 'There is *something* you can do, if you don't mind.'

'What?' His answer was sharper than he intended, but Luke was unfazed.

'The hotel. Can you arrange some-thing for the wedding night? No

15

— don't look like that. I want you to organise flowers and champagne for the bedroom. Roses and lilies. That's what she likes. And chocolates. Lots of chocolates. Get them to bill me for it.'

Joel couldn't help but laugh. 'You sly old romantic, you,' he said. 'You *do* love her, don't you?'

Luke flushed, just a little and Joel knew he'd struck a nerve. 'Go!' Joel said again, grinning. 'Leave it to me. I'll sort it out. I'll see you Friday night. Have our last drink, with you as a single bloke, and then get you tucked up for an early night.'

The colour drained from Luke's cheeks and he did look, just for a second, quite nervous. 'God,' he said. 'I hope she bloody turns up.'

★   ★   ★

Joel hadn't actually been to Carrick Park Hotel. He'd heard about it, and he had seen a brochure about it that Erica had given him; but he'd never set foot in the place.

He knew it was somewhere on the moors outside of Whitby. He lived a few miles south, in the newer part of the coastal town of Robin Hood's Bay. No doubt, he would have driven past the place — or past the little road that led up to it — but sorting out Luke's special request was a decent enough excuse to drive over to the hotel, and see where he was supposed to be going next weekend. It wouldn't take long and it was a nice evening, still warm, with a salty breeze freshening the air. He set up his sat-nav and climbed into the car, the roof rolled down on his silver Audi. He'd never regretted trading in his old VW for the soft-top, and days like this justified it even more. Summer time was absolutely the best time of the year, as far as he was concerned. It was great in Yorkshire, but even better in Cornwall . . . he shook his head. Pointless going there. Summer was great. He'd just leave it at that.

Idly, as he drove along the winding moorland roads towards Carrick Park, the sun warm on the top of his head, Joel pondered the amount of organisation that had gone into this wedding. He'd never really considered it as an industry before, but he was, after all, in advertising; he knew exactly how the companies would put a spin on things, so you felt like the only person in the world who didn't have a miniature, silver-and-white, specially designed digital camera on each table. Or that yours were the only guests who wouldn't have a hand-decorated, gift-wrapped Belgian chocolate heart, iced with the wedding date and initials of the happy couple to complement the hand-made, pressed-flower, embossed place settings.

It was all well and good, and he wished every couple who had their dream wedding the best, he really did. He just wondered if the whole idea of getting married had taken over from the idea of actual 'marriage'. It seemed to be a competition between brides to see who had the biggest dress and the most Cinderella-like Pumpkin Coach, with the most white horses dragging it to the biggest, most costly ceremony ever.

Just look at poor Erica. Last time he'd seen her, she was grey and haggard, stressing over when she could fit getting her nails done in between practice runs for her extravagant hairstyle and still ensure she had time left over to sort out individual wedding favours. But she couldn't, she had hysterically informed him, tie up the bloody ribbons for the favours with false nails.

And then there was Luke, coasting along in her wake, ready to turn up on the day and promise to love her forever. Joel wouldn't be surprised if she had a nervous breakdown at the reception, poor girl.

Was the whole wedding thing ever worth it? Just live together, for God's sake. What difference did a piece of paper even make?

He was cynical. He knew he was cynical.

He didn't really want to revisit his narrow escape of almost six years ago. He blanked it all out of his mind and kept an eye out for the discreet signs he had probably seen and not taken any notice of a hundred times or more. And there they were: *Carrick Park Country House Hotel*. He indicated right and turned in. Time to see what this country house hotel was like.

3

Rosa handed over a set of keys to a businessman who had a suitcase and a laptop bag with him.

'Turn right at the top of the stairs,' she told him, 'then go along the corridor and it's the fifth room on your right.'

The man smiled gratefully at her. 'It's been a long day,' he said, 'I'm ready to fall into that bed. I'm getting too old for conferences.'

Rosa smiled. 'Well your dinner reservation is for seven, so do you want us to give you a call around six-thirty, to make sure you're awake?'

The man laughed. 'That might not be too bad an idea. Yes. I'd very much appreciate that.' He loosened his tie, sweat beading a little on his forehead. 'And a cold glass of something with dinner would make it even better.'

Rosa smiled, and nodded, and made a note. 'Very good. I'll talk to you later. Enjoy your stay.'

'I'm sure I will.' The man trekked off up the broad staircase, past the big Victorian portrait of Lady Eleanor Carrick, which hung in the stairwell. Rosa watched the man go and her gaze drifted, as it often did, to the beautiful, fair-haired Eleanor. Automatically, she transferred her gaze to the bureau in the corner of the reception area, which held a few copies of a book a local author had written about Eleanor and her ill-fated marriage. Rosa needed to order in a few more copies of the book, and she made a note about that as well.

The books were tumbled in a bit of an untidy pile, which didn't make for a good impression so Rosa slid out from behind the reception desk and went over to the bureau, straightening the pile up and flicking through the book herself, as she sometimes did. She had read it countless times, usually on the very late shift. Some people thought

Eleanor haunted the hotel, and it was a nice tale, but Rosa, ever practical, had never felt anything untoward at all.

She preferred, instead, the factual, historical details of Eleanor's story; and if she ever imagined anything at all in those witching hours, it was only how many servants must have drifted around the Park to keep it up and running for the Carrick family. In her dreamier moments — which were few and far between — she sometimes considered how the place must have looked when it was filled with beautiful women in glorious gowns, sweeping down the stairs and through the corridors. On a summer's evening, a summer ball must have been a sight to behold — especially on a night like tonight when the roses were in full bloom and the trees were green and shady, just where they needed to be.

When the brides turned up to Carrick Park in their finery, Rosa sometimes caught the odd one looking up at Eleanor's portrait and possibly imagining themselves living here, as Eleanor had done. It was a pretty enough thought, and sometimes Rosa had whispered to the brides that Eleanor had been depicted in her wedding dress, and the bride she was talking to looked just as beautiful in their gown. It wasn't always true about the modern-day brides, but she saw them stand a little straighter, lift their chins a little higher and *believe* it to be true.

It was as she was straightening the pile, that she felt a draught on her back, which indicated that the big front door had opened, and sure enough, seconds later, footsteps sounded across the polished wooden floorboards.

Rosa turned, the professional smile on her face, a book still in her hand, ready to greet the visitor.

She felt the polished wooden floorboards shift and then her world tilted, just a little bit, on its axis. The book slipped to the ground and landed, open on the floor. She made no move to rescue it, vaguely thinking how Jessie would have slid, rugby-like across the floor to grab it before it landed.

Instead, she stared at the man who had just walked in. He, in turn, started and blinked, stopping right in the middle of the floor. His clear green eyes met her bright blue ones and she took in his tousled dark brown hair and coffee coloured T-shirt. He hadn't shaved, which wasn't surprising, because he had always suited that half-woken up, semi-shaved state. And why change the habit of a lifetime?

'Rosa?' His voice was exactly the same. He took a couple of steps towards her and leaned down. He picked up the book she had dropped and handed it back to her.

'Joel.' There was no question in her voice.

He attempted a smile. 'How are you?'

'Very well, thank you. But I'm very busy, so how can I help?'

He flashed a quick glance around the

empty reception area and she felt her cheeks flush.

'I want to arrange something for a wedding. Some champagne, and some chocolates, and some roses and lilies for the wedding night, if that's okay?'

The blood rushed from her cheeks as fast as it had coloured them earlier. She knew she must look white and pinched, which was the very last thing she wanted to look like in front of Joel Leicester. Not a good look at the best of times, and especially not good when most of the guests she'd seen today, and all the staff she'd spoken to, were looking cheerful and relaxed and sun-tanned.

'A wedding,' she said, thinly. 'How nice. Is it yours, by any chance?'

Joel's eyes burned into her for a few seconds too long. 'No. It's Luke and Erica's. You don't know them.'

'Well. It's not like we were together long enough for me to get to know your friends, is it?'

It was like that old Humphrey Bogart

film. Of all the gin joints, in all of the world and all that . . . Instead, Rosa's inward rant went something like this: *of all the bloody hotels in all of the whole sodding world, why the hell did he have to walk into mine?*

At least, she thought bitterly, it wasn't *his* wedding. Not like last time.

4

'You look great.' Joel knew it was a pathetic thing to say, but he hadn't really had a chance to prepare anything witty or more interesting.

'Thanks,' Rosa said, a little stiffly. 'Do you want to come over to the desk and we can sort out your friend's wedding?' She tilted her head slightly, sticking her chin in the air in that gesture he had found so endearing, yet also so maddening.

Joel shrugged. 'Sure.' He followed her across the hall, wondering when she had started working here. Whether she had been here all this time, or whether she had ended up here quite recently. So he asked her, more for the fact that it was a good way to fill the silence between them: 'What eventually happened with your job at the bakery?'

'The bakery closed down, but you

might have known that.' She slipped behind the desk and sat down at the computer. 'Donald and Anthony retired, and they couldn't find anyone else to take it on. It was a shame.'

'Didn't you fancy doing it?'

Rosa shook her head and tapped a few buttons on the keyboard. 'No. I would have needed a lot of capital, and a lot of experience. I didn't have either. I was happy enough doing what I did, just working for them.' She smiled slightly, but not at him. 'My baking's always been more about a hobby and feeding my friends than anything commercial.'

'Ah well, you know what they say,' said Joel. ''The heavier you are, the harder you are to kidnap. Stay safe and eat cake.' It's a pretty good advertising slogan.'

Rosa glared at him. 'I don't do it to make my friends fat. I do it because I like baking.' She transferred her con-centration back to the screen and clicked the mouse a couple of times.

'And anyway,' she remarked bluntly, 'you never complained about my strawberry sponge. When are Luke and Erica getting married?'

Joel felt the corners of his mouth lift. She was right — she'd packed a strawberry sponge for that trip to Cornwall and he was happy to realise she still remembered it too.

'It was a good holiday, wasn't it?' He lowered his voice.

Rosa looked at him. 'Cornwall? I loved Cornwall.' She looked away, back at her screen. 'Shame you came back to a squatter. Now — what was the date?'

'Oh,' he said, understanding the fond reminisces were over. 'This Saturday. It's getting close.'

'Ah yes. Luke and Erica. I've got them here. Luke Dresden and Erica Hall. Ailsa's been dealing with it all.' She slid him a wry glance. 'Ailsa is our Wedding Events Coordinator. You might have met her?'

Joel wasn't sure if Rosa was making a

joke or not. Her professional veneer hadn't shifted.

'I didn't meet Ailsa, no.' He wondered if that veiled comment had something to do with the fact Ailsa was apparently a wedding planner, but the very thought made him feel sick and he crushed it.

Rosa ignored him as she studied the booking system. 'Champagne and flowers and chocolates. It does sound lovely. Roses and lilies, you said.' Her face softened. 'Do you think she'd go for a bunch of rose petals in a basket to scatter into her bath? It's the perfect time of year. We can pick them from the gardens here.'

'Would you go for that?' he asked, almost without thinking.

Rosa's eyes narrowed slightly and she glared at him. 'Most girls would go for that, Joel, but as I don't know Erica as I never met her, and you *do* know Erica, you could perhaps hazard a guess?'

'Oh God — I'm not paying for it, and I know nothing, but Luke — ' He made a sweeping gesture with his arm. ' — Luke told me that he wants to make her day special and it's his idea so yeah, go for it. Rose petals in the bath. Don't suppose you do ass's milk and eunuchs as well, do you?' He gestured again. '*The Cleopatra Experience Wedding Package.* It might work.'

'I don't have any asps, sorry. Health and safety won't allow it. Okay. I've made a note and I've sent Ailsa the request, so she'll sort that out. Shall we bill Luke for it, then, if you're not paying?' She pressed a few more buttons. He saw that beneath her make-up she was pale, and her hands were definitely shaking as she typed something on the computer. She wasn't really *that* composed then. Ironically, that made him feel a little better. Why should he be the only one suffering in silence?

'Yes. That's what he wanted. Let's keep Bridezilla and Mumzilla out of this one.' He waited for her to make a comment, perhaps smile a little, but she seemed to have withdrawn into some sort of turtle-shell of professionalness. A shutter had come down behind her eyes and he cringed a little. She'd clearly given as much as she was willing to. Or able to.

He tried again to engage her; hoping, perhaps to see her smile again. 'Erica and her mum have been a bit . . . excitable.'

He waited for her to say something; ask a question. But Rosa wasn't reacting. He wasn't going to be able to draw the conversation out any longer. Instead, Rosa looked at him. She folded her hands neatly, one on top of the other and effectively shut him down. 'Anything else I can help you with today?'

Joel shook his head, oddly deflated. 'No. Not really.' Then he paused and he studied Rosa; noticed those beautiful, cornflower-blue eyes again, and remembered the fleeting relationship they had shared. She had been so lovely; so easy to get on with, and so cheerful. He wondered if she was still like that, beneath that prickly professional veneer. 'Unless,' he said, 'you fancy meeting for a drink after your shift? We could have a catch-up. It would be nice.' He had to throw it out there, he simply had to.

Rosa stared at him, then slowly shook her head. 'I don't finish until one o'clock in the morning.' Shut down. Definitely. He cringed again.

'Ah. Okay. Well, I might see you on Saturday then.' He smiled. It killed him inside. 'It's good to see you.' He wasn't lying. Still, she stared at him. He nodded and shoved his hands in his pockets. 'Bye, Rosa.'

'Bye Joel.'

Joel paused, thinking he might add to the conversation — say something else that might at least make her smile or soften or something; but, despite his job in advertising where he was never usually at a loss to come up with a catchy phrase or a damn good hook, as far as Rosa was concerned, he might as well be illiterate.

'I did try, you know,' he said, eventually. 'I tried to explain it all. I tried to tell you.'

'Maybe you didn't try hard enough.'

'I couldn't have tried any harder. And I think maybe you know that.'

'Maybe I do. But it was a long time ago and I don't even know if it matters any more.' She deliberately looked away and began messing with her keyboard, her lips compressed into a thin line.

Joel hovered for a moment more. He opened his mouth to say something more. Then he gave up, and walked out of the hotel.

5

Six Years Ago

Tangled limbs and sunburned skin. Setting sun and a long, lazy evening.

Joel raised himself up on his elbow and watched her; watched the eyelashes rest on her cheek like tiny, black spider's legs.

Rosa. Her name suited her; suited her pale, English rose complexion and her fair hair and her stunning blue eyes, the colour of the sky on a cloudless day.

She stirred and opened those eyes; smiled lazily into his and turned towards him. 'Hello.'

'Hello.'

They were in Cornwall, a snatched weekend away from life in general, and Rosa was a breath of fresh air after Iris.

'I'm glad your boss sent for leaflets.' He smoothed a stray piece of hair away from her forehead.

'My boss.' She laughed and shifted so she was more comfortably ensconced within his arms. 'Which one do you think's in charge — Donald or Anthony? Because neither one of them would appreciate me calling them 'Boss'.'

'I don't know.' Joel laughed. 'It seems to me that when you talk about them, they are almost interchangeable.'

'Comes with being together for so long, I think.' Rosa smiled up at the ceiling, clearly thinking about the men who ran the bakery she worked for. She turned her head and looked at Joel. 'Family history lesson. Donald is my godfather. When you do eventually meet them, remember that he's the slightly slimmer one of the two. He's also godfather to both my sisters as well. My mum grew up with him. He's like her best friend, I guess. If any of us had been boys, I think Anthony would have been the other godfather. As it was,' she shrugged, 'we're all girls.'

'Doesn't Anthony feel bad that he's not special, then?' asked Joel curiously.

'He is special. He's very special. They both say it's just a bit of paper and they can both share the job. I think by the time Angel came along, Donald was thinking Anthony might like a turn, but Anthony said it was tradition and why change it?' Rosa giggled. 'Regardless, I wouldn't call either of them 'Boss'. My uncles are retiring anyway. They were hoping I'd take over, I think. But, yes, I'm glad they sent me to collect the leaflets as well.'

Joel worked for an advertising agency — just a small one, called GrafixCo, and Rosa had burst in three weeks ago to collect some leaflets for a bakery. Joel had been sitting on the reception desk at the time — literally sitting on it, his back to the door, flirting with and getting nowhere with Chesca, the tawny-haired bohemian receptionist, who drank endless cups of black tea and wore ribbons threaded through her curls.

'I'll just go and check where your leaflets are, darling,' drawled Chesca in her cut-glass Kensington accent, and she'd disappeared through the double doors behind her.

Joel had watched her go, then turned to make small talk with the client until she came back.

In that moment, all thoughts of Chesca evaporated and he was entranced, completely and utterly, with the girl whose fair hair was flying loose from her ponytail, and whose blue eyes stared at him curiously.

He'd opened his mouth to say something remarkably witty and had closed it again, silenced by the thought that he might totally show himself up in front of the girl in black leggings, black boots and an oversized shirt, belted around her middle.

'Sorry,' he said eventually. 'Who did you say you were?'

'I didn't,' replied the girl. 'But I'm Rosa. Rosa Tempest. I'm here for the bakery leaflets — like I told your colleague.' She grinned, amusement twinkling in her eyes. 'Like you probably heard.'

Joel had scratched his head and laughed. He'd swung himself off the table and stood in front of her. She was a good six inches shorter than him, even in her high-heeled boots.

'Yes. I'm afraid I didn't work on that project, or I'd have been willing to deliver them to you. I can't resist a cake.'

'I'm a big fan myself,' she said. 'But when you work with cakes all day, sometimes you just crave a bacon sandwich. You know — to take the edge off the sweetness.'

'I don't know. The more icing, the better, as far as I'm concerned. Sometimes, though, a good old-fashioned pound cake has to win the day.'

'A pound cake?' Rosa perked up. 'I don't hear the term 'pound cake' much. Most people say 'Madeira cake' now.'

'How about this, then. What do you

reckon to a sour cream pound cake? That should be an interesting one for a cake aficionado.'

'Ha! Easy. You replace some of the butter with sour cream. It's American. So it's not, technically, a pound cake, is it? Because you haven't got a pound of everything in it — you've lost some butter to some cream.'

'Damn! You're too good for this game,' Joel had joked, and the girl had laughed. 'Tell you what — ' he couldn't quite believe he was saying it, but the words were out of his mouth before he could think. 'Do you want to meet up after work and discuss the quirks of cakedom a bit more? I'm not so good at baking the things, but I'm pretty good at eating them.'

'Why not?' Rosa had smiled, showing tiny little dimples. 'I've got a whole catalogue of baking stories I could regale you with. I've worked in the industry long enough.'

And so they'd met up, and so had begun a discussion about scones, and which was the best; a Devon cream scone or a Cornish cream scone. Joel had taken the view that so long as clotted cream was involved somehow it didn't matter, but Rosa had insisted there was a different way to serve each one. There was, they came to realise a few days later — after many heated debates, it had to be said — only one way to resolve it.

And three weeks later, here they were in Cornwall.

'I'm forever in Donald and Anthony's debt, at any rate,' said Joel, dropping a kiss on Rosa's lips. 'It's a shame we've only got one more day here.'

'I know.' Rosa sighed and sat up. 'Then it's back to my little old flat over the deli-café. I do like it there. But it's not *here*.' She drew her knees up and wrapped her arms around her legs. 'When I was little, I read a book called *Green Smoke* by Rosemary Manning. It was about a little girl called Susan who visited Cornwall on holiday and she met a dragon. R. Dragon, he was called, and he lived in a cave on the beach. And he used to tell Susan all these wonderful tales about his life with King Arthur.' Rosa turned to Joel and smiled. 'And he used to tolerate the tourists if they left him snacks as well. God I loved that book.' She shook her head and frowned. 'I have no idea where that book is now. In fact — ' she raised her finger and pointed at nothing in particular ' — I *do* have an idea. Bloody Jessie. My sister. She's got a treasure trove in her house. The whole attic space, more or less, devoted to books. I'm sure she takes the ones she particularly likes from her bookshop and adds them to her collection. And I wouldn't mind betting my *Green Smoke* is amongst them. She thinks we're stupid, you know.' She pulled a face. 'Anyway, my point is, that I wouldn't mind having a *Green Smoke* day. A Dragon Day.'

'A Dragon Day? So, where do you want to go? Joel asked, curious.

'Padstow, I think. I'm pretty sure that

was the beach R. Dragon lived at. And Tintagel, of course. Because we need to see King Arthur's castle — '

' — and King Arthur's teashop and King Arthur's pub and King Arthur's souvenir shop,' interrupted Joel with a grin. 'Maybe we can buy a plastic Excalibur while we're there.'

'Maybe,' agreed Rosa, half-seriously, 'and then we can visit Dozmary Pool, where the Lady of the Lake is supposed to be. Oh, and Jamaica Inn, on Bodmin Moor, because they aren't too far away from each other.'

'I thought Glastonbury Tor was supposed to be Arthurian as well,' said Joel, reluctantly shifting out of the bed and planting his feet on the floor.

'It is,' agreed Rosa, 'as are parts of Wales, I believe.'

'Maybe we could do them all.' Joel turned and smiled at her over his shoulder. 'Somerset and Wales and Cornwall. It's an excuse to travel isn't it?'

'Do we need an excuse?' teased Rosa.

'Can't we just see what's there?'

'We could. I don't have a problem with that. It'll be fun.'

'Fun,' agreed Rosa. 'Absolutely.'

★ ★ ★

They had their *Green Smoke* Day. Rosa became highly excited when they saw a black rock off the coast, which she swore was the Witch Rock from her book.

'Honestly,' she said, giggling, 'it'll come alive and turn into a Witch — I swear it!'

They hung over the cliffs listening to the sea roaring into Merlin's Cove near Tintagel, and gasped and laughed their way up the steps to the castle itself.

Rosa flung herself onto a grassy bank and lay like a starfish, not caring who saw her. She stared up into the cloudless blue sky and sighed. 'I don't want this to end. Cornwall is perfect; absolutely perfect.'

'Have we come to a decision on the

scones yet?' asked Joel, throwing himself down beside her.

'Nope.' Rosa shook her head against the soft, green grass. 'I think we'll have to agree to disagree on that one. Maybe we should just split the difference and go for a general clotted cream scone.'

'It's like I said, clotted cream has the edge, regardless.'

'I'll make a batch of scones when I get home,' promised Rosa. 'And we can do some intensive testing.'

'Can you throw a lemon drizzle cake in there as well?' asked Joel hopefully.

'I probably can. Come on.' She stood up and stretched. 'Let's go and see this castle and work up an appetite.'

'Good idea,' said Joel, and joined her. His hand sought hers and her fingers curled trustingly in his. It felt right.

6

They had one more night of sleeping in their little cottage, the curtains open against the black, star-speckled sky, candles lit around the bedroom and a bottle of wine half empty by the side of the bed.

The window was flung wide, the scent of saltwater and sharp grass floating through the night air. A tiny moth threw itself against the glass, too silly and too bedazzled to try and get into the house and head properly into the flames.

'I wish we could just stay here,' said Rosa with a sigh. 'But real life beckons I suppose.'

'Are you always this practical?' Joel laughed. 'Can't we just pretend this is it? This is real life?'

'I'd love this to be real life. Unfortunately, I'm usually far too sensible — but I'm not sensible enough to hide it. Sometimes it sucks being practical and people don't get it. I think I've been ruined by romance. There's nothing left to be, *but* sensible.' She sighed. 'And sometimes I even bore myself. I wish I was more like my sisters. They're a lot more fun and a lot more exciting than me.'

Joel reached over and took her hand. 'But not half as pretty and not half so clever, I bet.'

'They're pretty *and* clever!' Rosa laughed. 'One designs jewellery and one runs a bookshop. They'll both go far.'

'But can they bake?'

'Can they hell. That, my dear, is *my* talent.'

'It's a useful talent to have.'

'Shall we come back here again?' Rosa asked suddenly, throwing him.

Joel blinked. 'Yes, if you want to.'

'I think I'll definitely think about it.' She leaned forward and cupped his face in her hands. 'It's not very practical and not very sensible to plan that far ahead, but you know.'

'How far ahead are you planning?' teased Joel.

'I'm not sure. But as I say, I'd certainly like to think about it.'

★   ★   ★

So it had been quite a downer to drive home to Yorkshire from Cornwall, but it had to be done, as Rosa had said.

'Do you want to come back to my place?' Joel asked, not really wanting the time with her to end. 'Or do you want to go straight home?' He had a flat in Whitby in a clean-lined, modern block of six. Just one-bedroom, but it was enough for now.

Rosa clearly thought the same as him. Her hand crept over to his knee and rested there, warm against his skin. He was pleased he had chosen to wear denim shorts for the journey home.

'I don't want to go home yet. Let's go to your flat. It's closer to the bakery for work tomorrow and I'm already packed for a night away.'

'Is it really closer? And it works for me, if it works for you.'

'It is closer. And it definitely works.'

And so it was with a pleasant sense of anticipation that he parked his beaten-up old VW outside the block of flats and turned the engine off. 'Come on, then, Miss Practical. You only want to be here because it's close to work. You don't fool me.'

Rosa grinned. 'Damn, you guessed.' She stared out along the road and pointed. 'Donald and Anthony live just down that way. I'll surprise them tomorrow, I think, by getting to work first.'

'If that's what floats your boat. Come on. Let's get settled. I'm sure we can push to a takeaway tonight for supper, and I've got a bottle of white in the fridge.'

'Perfect.'

'Let me get your case.' Joel opened the door and got out of the car. He dragged their cases off the back seat and hauled them to the main doorway. They stood in the hallway, very close together. Then they got in the lift and stood together closer still.

By the time they had reached his doorway, they were both trying to hide their smiles and were ready to forego supper for a little while at least.

By the time they got inside and walked into the lounge, though, their relationship, Joel calculated later, was over.

7

'Joel. Where have you been? I've been here *ages*. Sorry, but I've opened the wine and I already had a shower. I didn't know when you'd be back, so I've sorted out dinner, and all *you* have to do is sit down, right next to me. Surprise!'

The girl was sitting — no, *lounging* — on the black leather sofa, her pink-satin clad legs curled up beneath her and magazines scattered all over the place. Her dark hair was hanging in two plaits and she had a face that, even scrubbed of make-up, was perfectly proportioned and artlessly beautiful.

Two other things struck Rosa, almost instantaneously. One, she had always hated pink satin pyjamas, and now she knew why; and two, the magazines were not just innocuous ones. They were bloody bridal magazines.

The third thing she noticed, which made her feel physically sick, was the huge, square-cut emerald ring, glittering mockingly on the third finger of the woman's left hand.

Joel froze and stared at the woman. 'Iris. What the *hell* are you doing here?'

'Reading my magazines. Getting comfy. Look. I've marked some things for you to read later.' She brandished a magazine, post-it notes stuck haphazardly in the pages and glared at Rosa. 'I could, however, ask what *she's* doing here. In *our* little love nest.'

'It's not our little love nest! It's my flat and I didn't know you still had a bloody key!'

Rosa didn't wait to hear any more. Numbly, she blanked out the angry exchanges between Iris and Joel and grabbed the handle of her suitcase.

This was far too close to home, far too reminiscent of what had happened with Jake. She was back there, back in the horrible flat above the off-licence, back after her shift at the bakery . . .

Back at the front door, turning her key in the lock. Back in the tiny hallway, listening to the feminine giggles coming from her bedroom. Her bedroom? Hang on. There were more noises — noises that she recognised far too well. Jake's excited heavy breathing; the woman's giggles turning into short, sharp, gasps, building to a climax as Rosa's knees buckled and her stomach churned.

She timed it quite perfectly, in retrospect — bursting in on them, just as they —

No. No. She couldn't go there again. She wouldn't go there again. God forbid that she, Rosa, should be the other woman this time. *No.*

Shaking, she backed out of the door; and once she was in the hallway, Joel's hallway, she ran as fast as she could to the staircase. She didn't even wait to see if the lift was there; she just hurtled down the stairs and burst out into the street. Then she turned left and bounced her suitcase all the way to

Donald and Anthony's house. There, she knew, she would find her refuge.

8

For God's sake, he thought he had made it pretty clear to Iris that it was over. They'd shouted a lot, she'd packed up what was hers and she'd walked out — straight to the car that was waiting on the road outside; and off she'd driven with some nameless lover Joel had never wanted to know better.

Then, a few months later, Rosa had swept into the advertising agency to collect her bundle of leaflets. Rosa who had made him laugh and agreed to meet him for a drink after work. Rosa, who'd instigated a *Green Smoke* Dragon Day in Cornwall and argued good-naturedly about scones.

Rosa. Beautiful, funny, uncomplicated Rosa.

'You left, Iris!' cried Joel. 'You walked out of here and you went off with — someone. We broke up! You gave up any reason you ever had to be here!'

'We did! But it was a mistake. It was a huge mistake, and now I'm back. We can try again, Joel, we had fun, didn't we? It's not too late to try again. I bumped into Paul downstairs, and he said you were due back from Cornwall today, so I thought I'd surprise you. Make it all nice for you coming home again — '

'It's far too late for any of that! I don't want you *here*, Iris! God, I should have changed the locks . . . '

'Don't be so stupid. You can't pretend you didn't miss me. *You've* done the rebound — clearly — and I've done it too. Joel, it just goes to show that it's not right if we're apart. I kept the ring — look.' She lifted her left hand and the emerald ring glinted off her third finger. 'We can try again. Seriously. I just thought if we could put the past behind us, we can pick up where we left off. You know — plan our wedding again. Properly.' She moved over to him, her arms outstretched, hoping, perhaps expecting, that he would take her in his own arms and all would be forgiven . . .

'Iris, are you for real?' Joel side-stepped her embrace, raked his hand through his hair and looked around him helplessly. This conversation was the result of one of three things: one, Luke had set up a video camera in the cupboard and they were all in cahoots to some horrific prank; or two, he had died and been resurrected in some awful, alternative reality Hugh Grant film. But then of course it might simply be number three; Iris was completely under the impression that she would be forgiven for cheating on him, and they could laugh it off. Drink that wine; fall into bed; all would be forgiven. *Oops, sorry. Just a teeny tiny mistake — it won't happen again, I promise.*

No. No, that wasn't going to happen.

And thinking about it logically, the Hugh Grant thing was, also, quite frankly, weird. Desperately, Joel considered option one:

'Luke? Luke? Get your arse *out* of my cupboard and show yourself!' he shouted. There was no answering sniggering, and no, *Mate! It's just a laugh! I could win two hundred and fifty quid if you play along. I'll split it with you!*

So, in light of no Hugh Grant weirdness, he had to finally, reluctantly, go with option three: 'Iris! Please. Just *stop*. It' not going to happen. We're finished. We're over.'

Then he suddenly remembered that Rosa was witnessing all this, standing quietly behind him. 'Rosa — ' he began, swinging around to speak to her. But she was gone.

9

'Hello.' There was no preamble. Rosa stood on her godfather's doorstep, her face pale and her emotions in check. 'Can I come in? I've been to Cornwall.'

'Of course, my darling girl.' Donald stepped back, clearly knowing better than to probe and Rosa walked on autopilot through the doorway.

She paused in the hall and turned to him. 'Can I put my case in my room?'

Each of the Tempest girls had a room at Donald and Anthony's. As children, they had spent a couple of weeks each summer there, being spoiled and indulged by their uncles. As adults, they spent the odd night; but their rooms had never changed — Rosa's was still the big room at the back, with a view over the rooftops right across to the sea. Jessie had favoured the little attic room with the rose-patterned sink in the corner, and Angel had squeezed herself into the tiny box-room at the front. Even then, Angel had a thing for small, cosy rooms tucked away in old houses. Jessie had told her, often, that it was like sleeping in a coffin and that Angel was weird for enjoying it.

'Of course, of course.' Donald closed the door. 'Would you like some tea?'

He looked so worried, that Rosa felt the tears build up behind her eyes. 'Yes please.' Her voice suddenly caught on a sob. 'I don't want to ring my parents. I don't want them to know the mess I'm in. Again. It's too embarrassing. I'm too stupid.'

'I'll go and pop the kettle on.' Donald patted her arm, and Rosa bit down on her lip hard. The last thing she wanted was sympathy and love. She knew she would just crumble in the face of that. She felt herself going when Nigel the Westie peered sleepily around the corner and suddenly began to bounce and bark, delighted to see her.

Fussing Nigel as he pranced around

her legs, Rosa eventually managed to sidestep him, and took the case upstairs. She put it on her bed and opened it up, shaking out her night-wear. The scent of the Cornish holiday cottage still clung to the clothing and she buried her nose in it, closing her eyes and trying to make sense of it all. How had Joel managed to keep a live-in girlfriend — possibly even a live-in fiancée — secret? Iris had certainly looked like she belonged there.

'Do you want your tea up there or down here?' shouted Donald from the ground floor. 'It makes no difference to me.'

'I'll come down for it,' shouted Rosa, her voice sounding thin and echoey in her old bedroom, still decorated with Disney Princess stickers on the window pane, a multitude of teddies piled up on the rocking chair, ready for her to choose one to take to bed with her.

'All right. Take your time,' replied Donald.

'I'll not be long,' she called. She

chose the tattiest, oldest, friendliest teddy from the pile and tucked him in bed, pulled on grey joggers and a grey vest top, then wandered barefoot down the stairs into the kitchen, where she hung over Donald as he made the tea and, unbidden, made her a honey sandwich on homemade bread — her childhood favourite.

'Thank you, Uncle Donald,' Rosa said in a small voice.

Donald looked at her, his eyebrows raised. 'Uncle Donald? My love, it's at least twenty years since you called me that.'

'You'll always be my Uncle Donald.'

'What's he done?' asked Donald, finally, it seemed, caving in enough to ask her questions. 'I'm assuming it's a boy. It can't be work — can it?'

He looked so sweetly guilty that Rosa shuffled over to him and hugged him. 'No, it's not work. I know you guys have to retire. I know you want to spend more time together.' Anthony had suffered a heart attack the previous year, and that had clinched the decision about closing the bakery. 'I've got something lined up. It's fine.'

'We wish you would take it over,' said Donald mournfully. 'It was always our dream.'

'It's not the right time.' A vision of Joel flashed across her mind and she felt sick and cold, all together.

In Cornwall, her change of job didn't even seem like a factor in real life. In Cornwall, everything was different. She could imagine she was a girl in search of a friendly dragon, and all that mattered was the next snack and a cosy bed in R. Dragon's cave.

Another treacherous sob caught in her throat and she was comforted to feel Donald's arms tighten around her. 'You're right. It's a boy,' she admitted. 'I could never fool you, could I?'

'Never, my dear. Come on now, tell me all about it. I can't pretend to have any of the answers, but I can listen.'

Rosa took a deep breath. 'It's Joel. We had such a lovely time, and when we got back to his flat, there was a girl there.' She screwed up her face. 'And I think . . . I think they're going to get married.'

'Oh, my!' cried Donald. He quickly stirred the tea. 'Let's sit down and discuss it.' And as good as his word, he picked up the tray and put everything on the island in the middle of the kitchen. 'Now — talk,' he instructed.

Rosa did as she was bid. Donald got the whole story — from her meeting Joel at the agency, to the instant attraction, to the holiday in Cornwall.

'I haven't even told Jess and Angel half of this,' she sniffled, blowing her nose for the umpteenth time in some kitchen roll. 'It's too embarrassing. Angel's at my place right now, while her damp proofing gets sorted. I've had to text her and warn her, just in case he comes over to lie his way out of it. And I've switched my phone off so he can't call me. I don't want to hear from him — ever. I'm done with him. I'm done with men in general. I'm supposed to

65

be the sensible one. I'm the one my sisters are supposed to look up to. And I'm so stupid! I've done this before — jumped into it on a whim and I've regretted it ever since; then I eventually find someone I actually *like*, and he's *engaged*! My love life is an absolute disaster.'

'I'm sure it's not, my lovely.'

'It *is*!' wailed Rosa. Donald tore off another sheet of kitchen paper and handed it over to her. 'God, I'm glad I've got a new job to look forward to at least.' She tried a wobbly smile, but it collapsed in on itself. 'I wish I could stay and work for you though. I wish things didn't have to change.'

Donald patted her and then pulled her close. 'There, there.' It was as if she was five years old again. 'I'm sorry. We're both very sorry.'

He looked so pained that Rosa shook her head and felt guilty all over again. 'No, it's not your fault. Not at all. I think I need a break from it all. I think it'll be good to start afresh, I really do.'

She took a deep, shuddering sigh.

'Well why don't you take the week off, and we'll say it's a holiday. Go away for a bit, back to your parents or to Jessie's place — or just stay here for a few days. Then it'll be time for your new job and we can draw a line under all this — '

'I'm home!' Anthony's voice carried through to the kitchen as the front door shut with its comforting thud, and the sight of him trundling cheerfully into the kitchen set Rosa off again. 'Oh my darling!' cried Anthony, swooping down on her. 'What a lovely surprise. But why the tears? What's happened?'

'It's a boy,' Donald informed him. 'Broken our girl's heart, he did. And he seemed like such a good one as well.'

Anthony shook his head in despair. 'We need to send you to a convent. I've always said that.'

Despite herself, Rosa managed a watery smile at Anthony's indignation. 'It's too late for that,' she said. 'I have a history, remember.'

'Nothing worse than any other nun, I would imagine,' said Anthony stiffly. 'I see you have tea and honey sandwiches. Anything *I* can get for you, sweetheart?'

'Just a big hug will do,' said Rosa. And as he wrapped his warm arms around her, she buried her face in his shoulder and gave in to the tears again.

10

He'd got rid of her — finally. There had been a lot more shouting and a lot more anger, but eventually, she had left — the engagement ring and the key were, at last, on the table, and he felt drained. He hoped this time she wouldn't come back, not ever. He'd made his feelings pretty clear and watched, exhausted, from the window as a taxi had pulled up and she'd stormed off into the night, fully clothed now, her satin PJs scrumpled up in the overnight bag she'd brought.

He tried to conjure up visions of Cornwall and Rosa sprawled on a bed, her cheeks flushed and a smile on her face, but that made him feel worse. Where the *hell* had she gone?

Joel threw the bridal magazines Iris had left in the bin — not even the recycling bin, the household waste bin, just to get rid of them — and, after calling the locksmith, just in case she had another key stashed somewhere, he tried to call Rosa.

'Tried', was of course the operative word. She hadn't picked up her phone; his calls were going straight to voice-mail. She didn't reply to texts and he didn't have an email address.

'Chesca, what have I got on today?' he asked the next morning, as he barged into the agency. 'Because I've got a very important client to see and I need to head straight out again. That bakery we did some work for. Rosa Tempest. It's an emergency. I might be gone all day.' He hoped he'd be gone all day. He *really* hoped that. He hoped she'd be at that bakery and they could sort it all out — then start again. Damn Iris!

'A client, you say?' Chesca blinked at him over her heart-patterned mug. 'Rosa? The Rosa you've just been on holiday with?' Damn Chesca! She wasn't as dippy as she seemed. 'Your client, your *Rosa*, will have to wait. Sorry. It's not in your diary, so — '

Chesca nodded in the direction of the back office. 'Pete needs to see you. He's in a total panic. He has a *real* emergency.' She smiled apologetically, her eyes honest. She leaned towards him. 'You *are* actually needed. Some damage limitation for the café down the road. They're selling 'pok pies' and 'naked beans'.' She pulled a face. 'Pete's proofreading failed, and he's got menus and things going out all over Yorkshire. I suspect your own . . . client . . . would be a lot more interesting naked than naked beans, though. I'm truly sorry.'

Joel's heart sunk. Pete was the worst exec in the place for fussing about. It would be ages before he got to the bakery.

★   ★   ★

He was right. It was late afternoon by the time he pulled up outside the little artisan bakery. He hurried into the building, hoping to catch Rosa.

'Hi, is Rosa here?' he asked the man behind the counter.

'Nope,' said the man.

Joel waited for more, but saw it wasn't forthcoming. Instead, the man folded his arms. 'Can I help you in any other way?' He smiled, and Joel saw, astutely, that behind the attempted-gruff exterior, the man appeared to be approachable and, more than likely, was one of Rosa's uncles. He wasn't sure if this gentleman was Donald or Anthony; but regardless, the pair of them obviously moonlighted individually as bodyguards for their niece.

Joel's stomach churned as he looked at the man. He knew Rosa must have said something to her uncles — but what she had said, and which one of her uncles this was, and what this gentleman was thinking about him, made him feel ill.

'No. Thanks,' replied Joel. 'I was really wanting to speak to Rosa.' He scratched his chin, realising he hadn't shaved this morning. God knew what he looked like after so very little sleep. 'I don't suppose you know when she'll be back do you?'

'She won't be back,' said the man. 'She's on holiday this week, taking a much needed break after a very, very disappointing *other* holiday.' He looked Joel straight in the eye. 'She came back to something she wasn't expecting at all.'

'None of us were.' Joel sighed. 'So will she be back next week? I'm sorry — I wasn't sure what you meant by her not coming back . . . '

'Exactly what I said. She won't be back, as we are closing at the end of this week.'

Joel felt the ground shift beneath him. 'Closing?' he repeated, stupidly. 'She said you guys were retiring — but I didn't realise the place was closing. I thought she was talking about later on . . . in the future. When she could take over . . . ' His voice trailed off, then rallied again. 'But she was collecting leaflets from my agency for you!'

'Yes. To thank our customers for their loyalty. Free cream scones on our last day. We are closing and she's moving on. We can't persuade her to stay.'

'But where's she going?'

'I can't tell you where she's going as she would never forgive me. And also it's all about the Data Protection Act.

'Oh — crap.' Joel could think of plenty more expletives, but he didn't think this portly, gentle-looking gentleman would appreciate any of them. 'Well if you do happen to see her, or hear from her, would you please tell her it wasn't what it seemed.' Joel focused on a Manchester Tart, dusted with desiccated coconut. It was easier than talking to the interchangeable uncle. 'Tell her that Iris and I are finished. That we finished months ago. Tell her I've changed my locks and told Iris exactly what the situation is. Tell Rosa I'm not engaged any more, nowhere *near* being engaged any more, and have no intention of being engaged to Iris at all again: ever. Tell her it was all a mistake and I'm sorry, and I'll be waiting for her call.' He dragged his gaze away from the tart and looked straight back at the uncle. 'Tell her all that from Joel. Please?'

The uncle smiled and softened visibly. 'You know, boy — Joel, yes? — I believe you.' He leaned on the counter and spoke softly. 'She needs time, you know. She's been burned before; and none of us want to see it happen again. Do you understand?'

Joel nodded. 'Thanks,' he said. 'I hope I'll hear from her.' He pushed his hands in his pockets and half-smiled at the man. 'I'm going to have to think of something else I can do — I really need to see her. And if that doesn't work, then it's up to her, I guess.'

'Good luck,' said the man. And Joel knew he meant it.

11

'Rosa, don't you ever make me do that again!' wailed Donald. 'You're one of our best girls and we love you unconditionally, but my goodness. I saw the pain in that poor man's eyes!'

Rosa scowled at Donald and folded her arms across her chest. She was enveloped in one of their aprons, an array of baking equipment scattered around the bench in their kitchen. 'I don't care,' she said.

'You should! He told me it was all a misunderstanding and I believed him. He looks like a very honest chap.'

'Looks can be deceiving. Perhaps his fiancée thought he looked trustworthy when they got engaged.'

'Oh Rosa! Give the man a chance!' wailed Anthony. 'Not every man is a Jake, you know?'

Donald nodded. 'I agree.' He began

to count off the points Joel had apparently made on his fingers. 'He told me to tell you that he and Iris are finished. That they finished months ago. That he's changed his locks and told Iris exactly what the situation is. He said he wasn't engaged any more, nowhere *near* being engaged any more, and he had no intention of being engaged to Iris at all again: ever. He said it was all a mistake and he was sorry, and he'll be waiting for your call. I think that was it, in a nutshell.'

'Nutshell be damned,' said Rosa. 'He's had time to think about it, that's all. We can all come up with a clever story if we're given enough time. It's only when you catch them at it, that they have no excuse.'

She saw Donald and Anthony look despairingly at each other and shake their heads.

'Darling girl,' said Anthony, 'won't you even reconsider it? Just chat to him and hear his side and see what he has to say. He tried to find you and explain. That's got to mean something, hasn't it?'

'It could mean,' said Rosa stiffly, 'that he's an even better liar than I thought. That he's a total chancer and I'm better off without him anyway.' She turned to the bench and gave something in a glass bowl a stir with a wooden spoon. 'I'm going to make coconut pyramids,' she said decisively. 'D'you want one?'

Donald and Anthony nodded their heads in unison, despite looking pained.

'Well of course we do,' said Donald, 'but we think you need to consider Joel as well.'

'Sod Joel,' remarked Rosa. 'I'm going to dip the pyramid bases in chocolate. That sounds nice, doesn't it?'

'It does,' said Donald with a sigh. He sounded defeated. 'It does indeed.'

Rosa stirred the mixture furiously, concentrating hard on the bowl. 'Good,' she said, and tried to quash any thoughts that invaded her mind which were not completely and utterly focused on coconut pyramids and the benefits of dipping them in chocolate.

12

He didn't quite know what else he could do — short of going to her flat and begging to speak to her, which is what he'd hinted at with the uncle. So that's exactly what he did.

Joel stood at the front door of Rosa's flat, by the deli-café window, and thought the mingled smells of garlic, wine and coffee had never turned his stomach more. He rang the doorbell for the third time, and heard the *click* as the door opened a crack, showing the staircase rising steeply upwards, behind a woman with a towel around her head and a scowl on her pale face.

'What is it? I'm *sick* of you sales people,' she snapped in a broad Scottish accent.

'I'm not a sales-person!' protested Joel. 'I'm looking for a friend. She lives here.'

'Here?' The woman opened her dark eyes wide and the ruby stud in the side of her nose glittered in the artificial light of the tiny lobby. 'I very much doubt that.' She turned and yelled up the stairs: 'Hamish! Is there a woman lives here with us? No? Thought not.' She turned back to Joel and folded her arms across her chest. She was wearing a huge, baggy, pale blue sweater and her legs were bare.

'A woman?' A male voice carried down the stairs, and the sound of footsteps came shortly after it. A tall man with too-long, mousey-brown hair appeared and stood behind the pale-faced woman, looking puzzled. 'What's she called?' His voice was even more Scottish than his partner's.

Joel swallowed, feeling rather foolish. 'Rosa. Rosa Tempest. I'm sure this is her flat. I've only been once, but — '

'Rosa!' The man looked at the woman, who turned around and stared at him. 'Isn't that the name of the woman we rented this place off?'

'Ah!' said the studded-nose girl. 'Yes. I mean, aye. It was.'

'Aye,' confirmed the man. The couple nodded in unison. 'No idea where she is. We just moved in.'

'Did she not leave a forwarding address?' asked Joel faintly.

The woman shook her head. 'No. Sorry.' She smiled, the expression brittle. 'Anything else?' She jabbed at her towel angrily. 'If I don't deal with it, it goes frizzy. The heat. The humidity. I need to diffuse — now.'

Joel spotted an intricate tattoo on the inside of the girl's wrist, which didn't really go with the pink fluffy towel and the outfit. 'Yeah. Sorry. Okay. Well, if she does come back, or if you hear from her or get any mail with a forwarding address, can you tell her that Joel called?' He pulled his wallet out and fumbled around, drawing out a business card. 'Can you get this to her please, if you *do* see her or hear from her?'

The woman plucked it out of his

hand and gave it a cursory glance. 'Aye,' she said shortly. 'Goodbye, then.'

'Goodbye then,' repeated Joel. He stood on the step until he heard the key turn in the lock. Then he walked back to the car. It was starting to rain. He looked up at the gathering clouds. Bloody typical.

★ ★ ★

'Mission accomplished!' said Angel. She looked at Zac and grinned. 'How was my Scottish accent?'

'Horrific.' Zac was Angel's best friend and always spoke honestly. 'You'd never win any prizes for acting.'

'I'm a jewellery designer,' said Angel, 'not an actress.'

'He didn't seem like a bad bloke, did he, though?' mused Zac.

'He seemed nice,' admitted Angel, 'but we have to go on what Rosa says.' She sighed. 'If that's what she wants us to do — get rid of him — then that's what we have to do.' She pulled a face.

'I do feel a bit bad, though.' She ripped the towel away from her perfectly dry hair and ran her fingers through it, pulling it straight. 'And here, you can have your sweater back too,' she added, starting to pull it over her head.

'No!' cried Zac. 'Please — keep it until you have your own clothes on.'

Angel sighed. 'Okay. 'Rosa's lucky that Goth Cottage has damp and we're here. But thank you for coming to see my workshop.' She smiled up at Zac. 'I know you hate the mainland. Sorry you couldn't stay at my place.'

'I do hate the mainland,' admitted Zac. 'I much prefer Skye. But I couldn't not visit when I was in the area, could I?' Then he grinned. 'But that was actually quite fun!'

Angel pushed him good-naturedly. 'We do have fun on the mainland sometimes, you know!' Then she sighed. 'But hell, I do feel sorry for that guy.'

13

Joel was at a loss. He'd tried her work; he'd tried her flat. He'd tried contacting her over all sorts of social media and wasn't having any success.

He sat at his desk in the office, devoid of creativity, and stared at his computer screen. *Green Smoke* and Cornwall seemed a long way away. There was nothing else he could think of doing. They had no friends in common, nothing he could use as a method of tracking her down. His gaze strayed to a box of paperbacks in the corner of the office someone had brought in to sell for charity, and then it struck him. There was perhaps one avenue left to him. Didn't she mention her sister had a bookshop? Jessie — that was it. Jessie Tempest.

A flicker of excitement sparked inside him and he opened up Google. He'd do a little investigation and see what he could come up with. And it didn't take him long to find there was a Jessie Tempest, Independent Bookseller in Staithes. That then, he thought triumphantly, was Saturday taken care of.

And sure enough, Saturday saw Joel trudging through a warm yet misty Staithes, a picturesque fishing village on the North Yorkshire coast, hunting out the bookshop he was positive was linked, even vaguely, with Rosa.

He saw the shop on the corner, splaying out prettily as if it was embracing the end of the terrace with its leaded windows. He pushed open the door and sniffed as the smell of ink and paper embraced him.

It was a strange shop, longer than he imagined it would be from outside and lined with shelving units full of books. Stands displayed art materials and postcards and stationery and local history books. One or two people were browsing the shelves and a blonde girl stood behind the counter, her hair the exact same shade as Rosa's, her eyes the same shade of cornflower blue. This had to be Jessie.

'Hello,' he said, approaching the girl with an encouraging smile. The fact she looked so like Rosa made him feel confident about speaking to her.

'Hello,' said the girl. 'Can I help?'

'Yes. I'm looking for Rosa. Rosa Tempest.'

The woman looked blank. 'Rosa Tempest?' She slowly shook her head. 'Nope. Sorry. Don't know her.'

'You must know her!' burst out Joel in frustration. He waved his arm at her. 'You look just like her!'

'And?'

'And,' repeated Joel, 'she said she had a sister who owned a bookshop.'

'Lots of people probably have sisters who own bookshops.'

'Her sister is called Jessie and she owns a bookshop,' said Joel. 'Please tell me it's you.'

'Why do you need to see this Rosa person?' asked the girl.

'Because I need to talk to her.' Joel gave up. 'She thinks something that is so completely outrageous, that I have to tell her the truth.' The girl raised her eyebrows, and Joel rushed in to fill in the gaps. 'She thinks I'm engaged but I'm not. My ex broke into my flat and Rosa saw her, and it all went wrong from there. My ex and I aren't together any more, and haven't been for ages. Rosa didn't give me a chance to explain. And she didn't hang around.' He cringed inwardly, remembering. Then he shuddered. 'Yes. So what I want — what I would love to do and what it seems I am being prevented from doing at every opportunity, is to see Rosa again and tell her the truth. She has to believe me. If I was guilty of anything, would I be chasing around the entire county to find some sort of link to her?'

'That *is* pretty outrageous. Both the Iris story and the chasing around the country story. But I don't know how you're going to get out of it, I have to say.' The girl looked down and shuffled some books into a pile. 'I would think this Rosa is generally a rather nice, forgiving type of person; but I would also think she's got some deeper reason to be suspicious of a man with a floozy in a flat. Especially when she thought she was in a relationship with him. Sometimes, people just need a bit of time to come around.' She looked up at him and fixed him with uncomfortably familiar eyes. 'You don't really know much about a person's relationship history when you've only been together a few weeks.'

Joel blinked. He leaned forward onto the counter. 'I never said she was called Iris,' he said quietly.

'Did you not?' she said blandly. 'I think you did. Anyway, I'm very busy, so you'll have to excuse me. I need to get on.'

'Right.' Joel was defeated. 'Thanks. If you do ever, at all, meet anyone called Rosa Tempest, would you be kind enough to tell her that Joel was looking for her?'

'If I ever do, I shall,' replied the girl, calmly. Her eyes travelled towards the children's' section of the shop. 'You might want to have a browse before you go,' she suggested. 'We have some lovely books in. And quite a rare one about a dragon, which is highly unusual.'

Joel paused. 'A dragon. Okay. Rosa had a book about a dragon when she was little. She loved it. Might it be that one?'

'It might be the same *title*,' said the girl, 'but it's not the same copy. I've no idea where that is.'

Joel nodded. This had to be Jessie — there was no doubt. He thought, also, that she knew full well where Rosa's book was and he half-smiled; although the entire situation was rather less than amusing.

'I'll check under M for Manning, then,' he said. 'Thanks.'

'You're welcome.' The girl turned away and busied herself with something on the desk behind her.

Joel paused for a moment, wanting to ask more; then he gave up. He went into the children's aisle and looked down the spines of the books. Sure enough, there was a copy of *Green Smoke*. He stared at it for a moment, his memory full of Cornwall and dragon caves and Witch Rocks on the beach. Then he plucked it off the shelf and took it to the counter.

'Ah, a good choice,' murmured Jessie Tempest. She rang it through the till and popped it into a sea-green paper bag, patterned with small cream polka dots. She handed it over to him carefully and looked him full in the eyes. 'Keep it safe,' she instructed. 'You never know.'

Joel's heart leapt. 'You never know what?'

'You never know,' said Jessie, 'how much these old books might increase in value over the years as they become rarer and rarer. Thanks again. Enjoy the rest of your trip.' She smiled at him politely and professionally and shut the till with the metallic ring of finality.

'Thanks,' replied Joel mechanically. He hovered for a moment more, then gave up and walked out of the shop.

The bell rang as he pulled the door open and stepped outside, clutching the bag. It was all a bit surreal. He looked at the bag and considered Jessie's words. He'd do as she suggested, he decided. No matter how long he had to keep the book, he'd make sure it was safe.

14

'Well I hope you're proud of yourself,' said Jessie, hands on hips, as formidable as a head teacher. 'He seemed like a very genuine, nice person.' They were in Jessie's ancient fisherman's cottage, just off Staithes High Street.

'Yes, he *seemed* like that,' said Rosa, 'but to find out he's got a fiancée tucked away is very, very *un*genuine and *not* nice.'

'He said she broke in. That they weren't together any more and it had been over for ages. He said he had searched all over for you so he could tell you the truth. And you know that's the case because we've all had to lie for you!'

'Lying is second nature to some people,' replied Rosa coldly. 'Might I suggest I look upstairs for a book that may have been misplaced?' She pointed

93

up towards Jessie's attic, a challenge in her eyes. 'My *Green Smoke* book. I haven't seen it for years.'

'No,' said Jessie. 'It's a mess up there and I need to catalogue everything.'

'I can help you.'

'No you can't. I doubt it's there anyway. I just wish that you had been in the shop today,' she continued, smartly changing the subject, 'then you might have bumped into him and saved me the grief. Where have you been, anyway? What brings you here? Even though it's too late for you to be of use to anyone.'

'I was just passing through. I was having a meeting with my new boss, and the hotel isn't too far away. It's one of those places that hosts bus trips a lot of the time, so it'll be busy and it'll keep my mind off things.' She looked down at her fingernails; short, neat and devoid of polish, because what use was having a French manicure to anyone who spent portions of their day up to their elbows in dough? 'I think it's time to reinvent myself as well. I'm going to get tougher and I'm going to start acting sensibly. And I'm not going to let any more men in. That's it. Once bitten, twice shy. Maybe twice bitten, thrice shy?'

'Donald-isms!' cried Jessie, clapping her hands and laughing. 'You've spent too much time with him. It sounded exactly like him as well.'

'Donald and Anthony have been *wonderful*,' stressed Rosa. 'I don't know where I would have gone that first night if they hadn't lived so close. I didn't have my car; I didn't have anything. And I still haven't told Mum and Dad.'

'That's a point,' said Jessie, pulling two mugs out of her little cupboard, and, almost as an afterthought, setting the kettle to boil. 'Our uncles will have to lie to Mum and Dad as well for you, will they? Just like me and Angel might have to if our parents ever ask about your stupid holiday and ask if we've heard from you at all. Well done, Rosa.

Well done. But anyway, what if Joel had seen your car outside your flat? What if *that* had happened?'

Rosa ignored the barbed comments about their parents and chose simply to answer about the car. 'Angel took care of the car thing.' She shook her head, impressed. 'The spaces are at the back, so Joel probably wouldn't have noticed anyway. But just in case, they brought Zac's car into my space and put mine up the side street, where his had been. Ingenious, yes?'

'Frighteningly so. But he'd never guess she was your sister. He had the measure of me, though,' Jessie admitted. 'We look too alike. But I did as you asked and headed him off at the pass.' She frowned and spooned coffee into the mugs. 'I felt so bad though.'

'No need to feel bad.' Rosa's mouth thinned to a petulant little line. 'He brought it on himself. And anyway, I'm not going to mention him again. I can't. It just brings it all back.'

'It's probably best to talk about it,

though,' suggested Jessie. 'You shouldn't really bottle it up.'

'I'm not bottling anything up,' snapped Rosa. 'I'm being realistic. I wanted to make a career out of baking, and I can't. I wanted to take over the bakery, and it's impossible. I can't let myself be the way I was with Joel, or the way I was with Jake. I just make bad choices. So it's time for me to do something useful with my career, and this new job at the hotel might just help with that. But I can't let myself get distracted.' She looked down at her feet. 'I'm going to be a new person. That's it. I've got to grow up and stop daydreaming. And I should stop believing in dragons and Camelot and expect someone to come along and treat me the way I deserve. I'm better off on my own.'

'I don't think you'll ever be on your own,' said Jessie softly. 'You'll always have me and Angel.'

Rosa forced a smile. 'Yes. Us Tempests have to stick together, don't we?'

'Even if we completely disagree with what you make us do?' fired back Jessie. 'Honestly, I think you're giving Joel less credit than he deserves.'

'Well maybe he should have just been honest with me in the first place,' snapped Rosa.

'And maybe you should have given him a proper chance.'

Rosa decided not to reply: it was an argument she doubted very much she would win. And that was something which she thought would be the case for a very long time; but she was a Tempest and she was stubborn and she doubted that she would ever change — no matter how many times she decided to reinvent herself and become a sensible, career-focused woman; instead of someone who, deep down, just wanted to bake cakes and have people love her for what she was.

15

Present Day

'Family conference,' announced Rosa. She was on the phone to Jessie. 'I need one. I know I don't normally ask for you lot to listen to me, but I need you to.'

'Okay. Skype?' asked Jessie. There was a faint grizzle in the background: Lottie, of course. 'I'll get Miles to do Daddy Duty and I'll sign in. Ten minutes?'

'Ten minutes is fine. Angel's just waiting to hear if we're good to go. I'll text her and let her know too.'

'Okay. Speak soon.' Jessie hung up.

Sure enough, ten minutes later, the three sisters were, sort of, in the same room. It was Friday teatime, the day before the wedding. Rosa felt a rush of affection for her younger sisters; Angel, dark-haired and dark eyed, Jessie, blonde and blue-eyed like she was. The three of them had scattered somewhat now, but technology was a wonderful thing and at least they could chat unhindered.

'Right. Like I told you, I don't normally need you guys to advise me, but I need to talk this through and need you to tell me something,' Rosa said.

'Jess, does it look like Rosa is perturbed?' asked Angel.

Jessie peered at the screen and leaned in a little. 'Yes.' She nodded. 'She looks rattled.'

'Rattled is the very *least* of it!' said Rosa. 'Can you remember Joel?'

'Joel. The one who had the squatter?' asked Jessie. 'The one after Jake?'

'We don't mention Jake!' snapped Rosa, her stomach churning at the thought of her ex, her absolutely biggest mistake — a mistake even bigger than Joel.

'Oh! Oh!' Angel waved her hands around. 'Joel! The one we all had to be mean to. The ex-girlfriend one — he was supposed to be engaged.'

'Ah!' Jessie shouted with laughter. 'Yes. And I still feel guilty about it! You broke his heart, Rosa Tempest.'

'It wasn't like that at all!' said Rosa. 'Stop making things up.'

'Gosh she really *is* rattled,' said Jessie. 'She's not neat anymore. I do believe she has a hair out of place.'

'A hair? Are you just jealous because Lottie is, like, intrinsically bald?' asked Angel.

Jessie snorted with laughter. Her daughter was so fair-haired she did indeed look bald.

'I wouldn't say she was bald, exactly, just that she doesn't have many follicles yet. But her hair will never be as neat as Rosa's. Was she always so neat?'

'Neat!' shouted Rosa. 'Stop it. Look. Joel came to the hotel the other day and he — '

'The hotel!' cried Angel. 'Oh wow. It's Fate. It has to be Fate. It's *definitely* Fate.'

'Shut up about Fate!' Rosa felt her cheeks burn as her temper rose. The warm rush of affection for her sisters was abating and for now and they were back in the nursery, two ganging up against one. 'Yes. Joel was in the hotel and he asked me to meet him for a drink.'

'So? Do you need us to tell you to do it?' asked Jessie. 'Because you should do it.'

'Definitely you should do it,' confirmed Angel. 'Fate and all that.'

'He just appeared there? That's actually quite romantic.' Jessie, nodded.

'Very romantic,' agreed Angel.

'He was never romantic. Never ever, beyond springing the Cornwall trip on me. But his friends are getting married at Carrick Park,' interrupted Rosa. 'And I said no to the drink, but it made me think.'

'You didn't go?' cried Angel. 'You idiot! Why didn't you tell us before?'

'I'm telling you now!' Rosa almost shouted. 'Look. It made me think, because what if I did the wrong thing last time? Perhaps he was telling the truth? Maybe I didn't give him a proper chance. Maybe,' she looked down and plucked a loose thread off her skirt, 'maybe I shouldn't have dumped him quite so rashly. What do you reckon?' She raised her eyes to the screen and was greeted by both sisters looking astounded.

'I don't actually know if it matters,' said Jessie after a moment. 'Because you did dump him and you can't change that. And you made us all be mean. Including poor old Donald and Anthony.'

'All I would say,' added Angel, frowning, 'is that it's Fate. I know you think I'm stupid and silly and airy-fairy and all that. But it might be, you know. Maybe now's the time for you to give it another go.' She shrugged, her white shoulders rising delicately under their gossamer covering of black lace. 'Fate.'

'Morticia is right.' Jessie pointed at Angel, calling her by the nickname

Kyle, her partner, had admitted to using when he first met her. 'How long has it been?'

'Six years, or thereabouts,' said Rosa. 'So much has changed though. I'm not the same person I was then. The 'me' now wouldn't have dumped him. The 'me' now would have got the truth one way or another and been certain that it *was* the truth. Perhaps it *was* all true — perhaps they had once been together, and they weren't any longer? So I do actually feel very . . . rattled.' She sighed. 'What do you think? I'm now wondering if I overreacted in the first place. You know how sensitive I am about weddings.'

Jessie, possibly the second most sensible of the Tempest sisters after Rosa, shook her head. 'I would say,' she said carefully, 'that if he's reappeared, it's maybe a good opportunity to try and rebuild things. What happened after you left him?'

'I never spoke to him again. Other than that, before that, we had a lot of fun.' She smiled suddenly, remembering. 'He loved my cakes — even the disasters.'

'Well a man that loves cake disasters is worth giving a second chance to,' said Jessie. 'I don't even know why you're asking us for our opinion.'

'I just — don't want to jump back in again and leave myself open to it all failing,' Rosa admitted. She had never accepted failure, ever.

'What does it matter if it *does* fail?' asked Angel. 'You know, Rosa, you do need to have some fun. What else do you do with your time?'

'I work,' said Rosa. 'And I bake.'

'And who gets the cakes you bake?' asked Angel.

'My colleagues.'

'Your colleagues at work,' said Angel. 'So — who do you socialise with? Outside of work.'

Rosa thought for a second. 'I don't really socialise.' God, that sounded depressing when she said it out loud. 'I work weird hours.'

'So, looking at this on a very basic level,' said Angel, inspecting her black nail varnish, 'it's not going to be easy for you to find a man is it?'

'I don't need a man to define myself!' cried Rosa.

'No, no, I agree,' said Angel, 'but maybe at some point in the future, you might want to actually *be* in a relationship?' She fixed her eldest sister with a Tempest Look. 'Joel's good enough to practice on if nothing else — and you already know him, so why not give it another chance? With no Iris to think about. Surely it would be nice if someone was around occasionally to cook you a meal?'

'Just have some fun,' chipped in Jessie. 'Fun is good. I mean — '

'Mum? Who are you talking to, Mum? Oh — hello!' A tousled, fair head appeared on the screen next to Jessie, then pushed itself to the front. 'Angel! Rosa! Hello!'

'Hello, Elijah,' said Rosa. 'How's the wasp sting?'

'Not bad, thanks. The vinegar worked.' He grinned into the screen. 'What are you talking about?'

'Cakes,' interceded Jessie quickly. 'Rosa is going to bake a fantastic cake and post us some. Aren't you?'

'Like last time? With the cider cake? That was soooo nice.' Elijah grinned again.

'Yes. Cider cake,' said Rosa. 'I'll post a slab down to you. The greaseproof paper and the cardboard box worked quite well last time, didn't it?'

'Yes it did! Thank you, Rosa!' replied Elijah. He turned and put his arms around Jessie. 'Mum, I need some help with my homework and Daddy is rubbish, so . . . '

'I'll be there soon,' promised Jessie. 'Now go and get it ready.'

'Okay. Bye!' Elijah released Jessie, waved at Angel and Rosa and blew a kiss. Then he placed a kiss on Jessie's cheek and scurried off towards a heavy wooden door behind her.

' 'Mum'?' asked Angel, raising an

eyebrow. 'Since when? I thought he called you 'Jessie'?'

'Hmm.' Jessie looked over her shoulder to make sure Elijah had left the room, then leaned forward. 'Since Lottie came along. He said it wasn't fair that his new sister would get to call me 'Mum' and he had to call me 'Jessie'. We just let him talk himself into it. It was his decision.'

'But what did Miles think?' Angel's eyes were wide. 'With Elijah's real mum being dead and everything?'

'Yep. I never wanted to take Libby's place.' Jessie frowned. 'But she died when he was two, and hopefully I can be a mum to him for a lot longer. So Miles was great. He said just to let him do what he felt was right. It's Elijah's choice. He knows I'm not biological — but I must admit I do love hearing him say it.'

'It's so lovely,' replied Angel. 'He's a nice kid.'

'He is indeed.' Jessie smiled at her sister.

Rosa was silent. Hadn't Jessie taken a leap of faith with Miles? Hadn't she stepped willingly into a relationship haunted by Miles' dead wife? A dead wife who had been pretty gorgeous-looking as well, by all accounts. Joel's tenacious ex was no comparison to a plaster saint, though. She sighed under her breath and slid her gaze across to Angel — beautiful, scatty, eccentric Angel. She'd given a man she originally hated on sight a chance, and look how happy they were.

Rosa knew, deep down, that playing safe was maybe not the way forward with this one. Iris was a long way in the past. And the thought of having someone there to boost her up after a long, lonely night shift was quite appealing on some levels. God, she'd sometimes kill for a cooked breakfast and a hot bath ready for her when she got in, but she'd never admit that in a million years.

'I don't suppose it would harm

anything to see how it goes, would it?' Rosa asked.

'It wouldn't harm anyone,' said Jessie quietly.

'It's Fate, my love,' added Angel. 'You should just embrace it; and you know where we are if you need us.'

'I'm sure you'll find me first, if you need me,' replied Rosa, a little wryly.

'We will!' said Angel.

'Yep. We always do!' said Jessie.

16

Rosa cursed the rota she had drawn up so carefully, ages ago; as she had feared, she was working day shift, on the Saturday of the wedding, which meant that there would be no escape from Joel. She'd talked herself in and out of trying again so many times she was absolutely dizzy.

Rosa had worked plenty of wedding days; during those events, the corridors of Carrick Park were always full of distracted bridegrooms, hyper brides, fraught colleagues and laidback best men, eyeing up the bridesmaids. She would almost rather take her chances with the so-called ghosts. This wedding was going to be a special kind of awful though — Joel would be around, and she would have to see him and speak to him and pretend she'd made the right decision by fending him off when he'd asked her to go for a drink. No. She *had* made the right decision. Of course she had. She couldn't forget that the last time she had agreed to go for a drink, they'd ended up as a couple and decamped to Cornwall for a long weekend.

Despite her resolve, however, Rosa found it was like poking your tongue into a painful tooth cavity. Therefore, on the day of the wedding, she found herself staring at the booking system icon on the screen and, before she could stop herself, clicking into it. She searched for his name: *Joel Leicester*. Her heart somersaulted as she saw it flash up on the screen.

As she had already suspected and dreaded, he was definitely here; he was actually in this building, right now. He was in a twin room and the somersault turned into sickness as she clicked further into the system. Was he still with Iris, after all that? Or was he with another woman? He would be perfectly entitled to be, but part of her didn't want to admit that. She had been practically celibate since they had split up. In fact, her resolve had never wavered in all the time they'd been apart. *Once bitten, twice shy* as Donald had said. Well, she had already acknowledged that she was twice bitten and would probably be chewed up and spat out if she let anybody else in.

So she wasn't quite sure why she felt so relieved when she saw the name of his room-mate: *Luke Dresden*. The Groom. Of course. It made sense. She closed the screen down. He was taking his duty seriously enough to make sure his friend turned up on the day. Ironically, he seemed to be doing a better job of managing Luke's wedding than he'd done of managing his own.

17

Meanwhile, Joel had slipped out of the room he had shared with Luke. Luke was talking about getting ready and not doing much about it, so Joel decided to leave him to it: no distractions, nobody to chatter to. Unless the Carrick Park ghosts decided to show up.

It was the thought of who would be the most terrified in that scenario that amused him, and the idea of Luke coming face to face with Lady Eleanor from the painting saw him smiling to himself as he wandered down the corridor, intending to go outside and have a walk around the grounds. It was a beautiful summer's morning. Maybe he could get a coffee and take it outside in the gardens.

'Excuse me — you're the best man, aren't you?' A small, highly official looking woman blocked his path. She had an iPad clutched to her chest and an expression of sheer horror on her face.

'Best man? Yes. If it's for Luke and Erica, then indeed I am that man. What's up?'

'Oh thank goodness I caught you!' The woman held out her hand and shook his briskly. 'I'm Ailsa, the Wedding Events Coordinator. We've got a problem and I need to check some details. Can you help?'

'A problem?' Joel involuntarily took a step backwards. In his head, Iris had turned up in a white dress, and claimed she was getting married as well, in some hideous ceremony he knew nothing about. It was exactly the sort of dream he'd had on and off, ever since he and Rosa had broken up.

'Yes. I'm afraid Erica is pretty upset,' said Ailsa. There were little grooves down the side of her mouth as if she was trying hard not to scream. As if on cue, a howl of anguish echoed around the corridor.

'Good God!' exclaimed Joel. 'What the hell is that?'

'That is the bride,' said Ailsa in a stiff little voice. 'As I said, she's quite upset.'

Joel clamped his hand over his mouth, terrified that he would laugh inappropriately. 'What on earth is the matter? If it's any consolation, you can tell her that the groom is here and is fully intending to turn up to the ceremony. And I'm here. And at least four of her bridesmaids are here, because I've just seen them along there.' He waved away towards the other wing of the hotel where he had seen four women in long dresses, shrieking and giggling. He had vaguely recognised two of them as Erica's friends.

Ailsa shook her head. 'I don't think any of that was ever in question,' she said, and Joel felt dampened. Whatever was going on, it seemed that humour wasn't going to lift the atmosphere much.

'Then what is it?'

'It appears that there's no cake.'

'No cake?'

The pair of them stared at each other for a moment.

'But she had spreadsheets,' offered Joel. 'And so did her mother.'

'Yes. I've seen the spreadsheets. In fact, I've seen the spreadsheets many, many times. However, both spreadsheets had the box for 'cake' ticked. Yet it seems that neither one of them actually arranged the cake. Erica has just announced that her day is, and I quote, 'ruined, completely ruined'.'

'Oh dear. Ruined, she says? The lack of cake is quite . . . surprising. Erica is a pretty organised woman.'

'So is her mother,' said Ailsa. They looked at each other and Joel understood, without that statement being qualified, that a 'Mumzilla' was indeed a definite entity in this wedding.

'And what can I do about it?'

'I just want to know whether you think, by any stretch of the imagination, that Luke organised a cake?' Ailsa looked at him pleadingly, her professional veneer slipping off her like a mask. 'Please. Please tell me Luke organised a cake?'

'Oh God. No. No, I'm sorry. Luke had very little to do with anything, to be honest. He organised flowers and stuff for tonight, but as far as anything else goes — he pretty much left it to Erica and Mumzilla. Sorry. To Erica and her mother.'

Ailsa nodded, the colour draining from her face. 'I'll have to see what I can do, then.'

'Let me see what I can do as well,' said Joel. A plan was forming — but whether it would work or not, he didn't know.

'Please,' said Ailsa. 'Please do!'

18

'Rosa! I was hoping it would be you.' Rosa looked up as Joel came rushing over and halted before the reception desk. 'I need to speak to you. I don't know if there's anything we can do about it, but there's a problem.'

'Joel!' Rosa looked up at him, trying and failing not to let a blush colour her face. She had just been thinking, again, of how much harm agreeing to a quick drink really could be. Her mind was somewhere in Cornwall, looking for dragon caves and on top of that, she felt as if she was balanced on a pair of kitchen scales, tilting in between 'Have a drink' and 'Don't even go there'.

'It's the wedding,' stated Joel.

'The wedding? Erica and Luke's wedding?' Joel nodded and looked amusingly pained. Rosa reached across for the phone. 'Do I need to call Ailsa? She should be around the hotel. In fact, she should be pretty close to Erica.'

'No — Ailsa already knows. She's trying to sort things out at her end — which means calming Erica down. She's bloody hysterical.'

From somewhere behind a closed door, Rosa heard a strangled wail; she raised her eyebrows to Joel. 'Is that her?'

'Yes,' he said. 'She reckons her day is ruined.'

'Ruined? But you said she was super-organised. Nothing can go wrong. She's Bridezilla. And you said she had a Mumzilla too?'

'Yes. But unfortunately, Bridezilla thought Mumzilla had done it, and Mumzilla thought Bridezilla had done it. There was a tick in the spreadsheet box. But nobody did it.'

'Nobody did what?' Rosa looked confused.

'Ordered the cake. This wedding is cake-less.'

'*Cake-less?*' cried Rosa. 'That *is*

120

pretty bad, but it's not going to ruin the day, surely?'

'It's ruining it,' said Joel, seriously; but there was a twinkle in his eye and a smile beginning to tilt his lips. Rosa was reminded of seeing that twinkle against a backdrop of blue sea and blue sky. 'It's not funny is it?' he continued. 'It's not actually funny.'

Another yowl came at them through the corridors of the hotel and Rosa covered her mouth with her hand. She had a horrible feeling that she was going to start sniggering too. And really, it *was* awful. But it was quite comical too, in a way.

'It just proves that you can go all out for these things, be super-organised, and still have an oversight,' she said. She took a deep breath and drummed her fingers on the desk, staring at Joel without really seeing him. There might be *something* she could do to salvage the day. She'd do it for any couple, not just a couple who were friends with Joel, and most certainly not because

Joel had asked for her help. Because that would be like giving in and admitting she might have been wrong about him six years ago.

She might regret this, but she had to at least try it.

'Okay.' She stood up decisively. 'How many guests has she got coming?'

Joel looked blank. 'I have no idea. Sixty? Seventy? A hundred? Luke never said.'

'Probably,' Rosa replied drily,' because Luke didn't ask. Now — I want you to go and find Ailsa and ask her to come and see me. I don't think it's insurmountable — I just need to pull some strings.'

'Okay. Will you be here?' He gestured at the fact she was standing up.

'Yes. I just need to get some cover for Reception, but I'll wait until I see Ailsa before I head off.' She turned her attention back to the telephone and dialled an extension. 'One of the admin staff can pop over and cover for a bit. I'll bribe them with chocolate brownies.'

'Thanks Rosa.' Joel smiled at her in that way that used to make her weak at the knees — before Iris had appeared, of course.

Rosa dragged her gaze away from him, determined not to let *him* see how rattled she was.

Joel's voice broke into her thoughts. 'Do you need me to drive at all? Does your godfather, by any chance, still have links to a bakery anywhere? Can we get a display model or something?'

Rosa shook her head, her eyes drawn back up to him, much against her better judgement. 'No. He properly retired. Go and find Ailsa. I'm still thinking.'

'Okay. I'll be as quick as I can.'

She nodded and waited for the Office to pick up the phone, watching Joel break into a bit of a jog to go and find the wedding planner. His dark hair had looked even more tousled this morning, and, horribly, it made him look even more gorgeous. He made the jogging look effortless and she stared after him, long-buried feelings most definitely threatening to surface.

Have a drink. Don't have a drink.

'Amy!' Rosa was thrown out of her own indecision as the call connected, and she was forced to look away from Joel's retreating back. 'If I offer you brownies, will you do something for me?'

'So long as it's not covering Reception. Even *your* brownies can't tempt me into that.'

'Brownies and oaty flapjacks?'

'Not unless the flapjacks have chocolate chips in them.'

'It can be arranged,' said Rosa.

Which meant it wasn't long at all before Amy was installed on the reception desk, grumbling slightly but willing to sacrifice herself for the sake of baked goods.

'Thanks Amy. You know where everything is, don't you?'

Amy nodded and tapped in her password. 'Unless anything's changed over the last few weeks, I'm good to go. If I get stuck, I know where you are.

And you owe me *big* time.'

'Thanks.' Rosa frowned. 'I'm confident about the brownies and flapjacks, but I'm not entirely sure about what I'm planning — but I've got to try it.' She looked along the corridor and waved as Ailsa and Joel came hurrying along. Rosa walked towards them, heading them off at the dining room door.

'My God, she's hysterical!' said Ailsa, by way of a greeting.

'Hmm. I had heard the screams,' said Rosa. 'The wedding is cake-less, I believe?'

'Entirely cake-less,' agreed Ailsa with a nod. She looked at her iPad and typed some things in, swiping the screens around. 'I was wondering if I had anyone I could call on in a hurry, but everyone seems to need a lifetime to create one bloody cake.'

Rosa smiled. 'Not necessarily. Can *you* tell me how many people she's got coming? And when do you need the cake?'

'There are fifty people all together, including the bridal party,' replied Ailsa, without hesitation, 'and the reception is due to start at two-thirty. So we'll need a cake by three-thirty, I would say.'

Rosa nodded. 'That's fine. Go and tell her it's under control.' She took a deep breath and turned to Joel, part of her hating that she had to ask him, and part of her wanting to trust that he'd do it. 'I don't suppose you could give me a hand, could you? I could do with some help, or this might all fall to pieces'

'Anything. Luke's my best friend — it's his cake-less fiasco as well as Erica's.'

'Then come with me.'

He smiled and lowered his voice, leaning in towards her. 'Is that a threat or a promise?'

Her knees threatened to buckle, but she forced herself to remain professional. 'Depends on your wrist action,' she said briskly.

19

'Wrist action'. Joel couldn't help laughing in a shocked sort of fashion when he realised where Rosa was leading him.

'The kitchens,' he said. 'Don't tell me. You're going to make the cake.'

Rosa shook her head and took her jacket off. 'I'm not. We are going to make at least fifty cakes. Too much pressure on making one big cake for that size of event, especially if it's a wedding. I'll do one biggish Victoria sponge for them to cut, and it'll look fine. What's her colour scheme?'

Joel thought for a moment. 'Lilac and silver,' he said. 'The bridesmaids' dresses were in that colour anyway.'

'Close enough,' said Rosa. 'We'll go for that.'

'When you say at least fifty cakes — ' he looked around them, 'what do you mean?'

'Cupcakes,' she said. 'Very fashionable and very easy. We can cook them all as basic sponges and then decorate them.' She reached out to unhook two aprons from behind a door.

'But don't you have catering staff?' Joel asked, looking around at the spotless, yet rather empty, kitchen. 'They'll be upset if we start messing around.'

'We do have catering staff, but they went home after the breakfasts, and we don't get the next lot in for an hour or so.' She gestured with the apron. 'Which is why I need your help. We will not be messing around. Now, put your apron on.'

Joel tied up the apron and watched Rosa deftly tie hers; then she went over to the cupboards, where she began hauling out flour and sugar and vanilla essence. 'We need butter and eggs and milk,' she told him, pointing to where he might locate them, 'and icing sugar — ha! Plenty here. That's good. Buttercream always takes more than you think. Right, so for twelve cakes, I need four ounces of butter, four ounces of sugar and four ounces of self-raising flour. And two eggs and about two tablespoons of milk. And a teaspoon of vanilla.' She waved the brown glass bottle at Joel. 'So how much do we need for, say, sixty? So we can have some disasters and some testers and nobody would know?'

She was suddenly every inch a professional chef, very different from the Rosa he'd known in Cornwall, but definitely coming into her own in this huge kitchen.

He also understood the question was more than likely rhetorical, but he did ask, 'Why ounces? I thought you'd be all metric by now?'

Rosa shook her head and hunted for a pen and paper.

She settled on an order pad and quickly jotted something down. 'My gran used ounces, Donald and Anthony use ounces. I'll use ounces as well, thank you very much. Right. If I multiply it all by five?' She looked up and asked the question of Joel; but again, he knew it didn't require an answer.

'Yes,' she continued. 'By five. So . . .' She scribbled something else. 'Let's start with twenty ounces of the dry ingredients and ten eggs. Five teaspoons of vanilla and ten tablespoons of milk. Great. Get a big bowl, will you? They're over there. And a sieve. I'll start weighing them out.'

Joel did as he was bid. He had tasted Rosa's cakes before and knew that she could nail this; even if the purple food colouring she was gesticulating at looked a bit foul.

'We'll have some with lilac icing and some with white and some with silver balls on and — oh! Flowers. Edible flowers.' She paused, the flour jar tilted at a dangerous angle over the scales. 'Lavender and rose petals. That would be nice. There's a gorgeous purple rose just in the walled gardens — we could use that. Yes. If you go and collect some of the flower heads, while the cakes are cooking, that'll be great.'

The day was, Joel knew, turning out to be a beautiful one. The sky was bright blue and it was already warm with just a whisper of a breeze to tickle one's skin. The garden would be perfect; sheltered and scented with summer flowers. Ideal for what Rosa envisioned.

Joel beat the eggs as Rosa creamed the butter and sugar, then tipped a little into her bowl at a time. As Rosa stirred in the vanilla extract and transferred the flour into the bowl, Joel went in search of cake tins and paper cases, and dropped them in to the baking tin, one at a time. By the time he had finished, Rosa had the mixture ready to pop in the cases.

Soon, the little cakes were in the huge ovens, rising nicely.

'I can't thank you enough for this,' said Joel.

'It's the simplest solution.' Rosa was busy weighing out icing sugar to prepare the buttercream. 'I'll do a couple of drops of colour in a batch of this to see how it goes — I can always add more, but I can't take it away. Good God, fifty ounces of icing sugar. I'll get marmalised by the Chef.'

'Or caramelised?' suggested Joel.

'Or caramelised,' agreed Rosa. 'There, that should do it.' She put the icing sugar jar down and a little cloud of it puffed out of the top. 'Okay — do you remember which flowers to get?'

'Rose petals and lavender. I'm on it.'

Rosa nodded to the fire exit. 'Go out that way and follow the path around. The walled garden is just along the way. You'll know the rose when you see it. It'll be in full sun by now and smell divine. You can't miss it.'

'Great,' said Joel. 'I won't be long.' He grabbed hold of her and pulled her towards him. He kissed her, swiftly, on the lips. 'I mean it you know. Thanks.'

This time, a heady flush swallowed Rosa up, her cheeks the colour of a summer sunset. 'You're welcome. Now go and pick flowers. I've got a Victoria sponge to make next.'

'I'm going,' he said. And kissed her again for good measure.

★   ★   ★

By the time Joel came back, five trays of a dozen, golden cupcakes were lined up; the kitchen smelled of vanilla and baking and a warm, sweet heat, and he could see one of the ovens contained two tins with pale golden domes just cresting the top of them.

Rosa jumped off the bench where she had been sitting and went over to greet him. 'Don't let them know I was sitting on the bench,' she said. 'I'll wash it down, I promise. I made some tea as well. You can't have cakes around you and not have any tea to hand.'

'My lips are sealed. And tea sounds good. Are these okay?' He held up his hands, and rose petals and lavender heads spilled out.

'Perfect.' Rosa leaned down and closed her eyes, inhaling deeply. 'Gorgeous.' Carefully, she took the flowers, still warm from the sunlight, from him and their fingertips brushed against one another. Alarmingly, she felt herself spark at the touch and quickly continued the conversation. 'I'll separate all the petals out and get everything iced when the cakes have cooled.' She looked up at the clock. 'It's probably time for you to get ready anyway. I don't think the wedding can be best man-less as well as cake-less.' It was one way of getting him out of the kitchen, anyway. She was still tingling from the mere touch of his fingertips. God knew what she would do if he lingered any longer in a deserted kitchen with her.

Joel followed her glance. He'd picked up the mug of tea she'd prepared and now he quickly drained it. 'Yes. I should probably get a shower. If I look anything like you — ' he gently tucked a strand of sticky, cake-mix covered hair behind her ear and rubbed his finger against her cheek where a smear of icing had found its way, ' — I'll need a proper scrub down.'

'You most certainly will do.' He was too close; far too close. 'You've got cake mix on your face as well.'

'Have I?' He put the mug down and rubbed away at his own face; Rosa longed to feel his warm skin and prickly stubble beneath her own fingertips, but instead she turned and dumped the flowers in the sink, determined not to look at the dusting of icing sugar that had somehow found its way into his messy, tousled hair.

'I'll just give these a wash, because I don't want to serve greenfly to you guys. Leave it with me and I'll see that it's all ready for Erica and Luke at the reception.'

She turned the tap on, knowing that Joel was still hanging around the kitchen. Determinedly, she began to wash out the petals, running them under the water, and trying hard not to look at him.

'Thanks again,' he said. 'I'll see you later, yes?'

'Yes. I'll see you later.' She turned and looked up at him, catching his eyes and blushing again. Now the practicalities and concentration of baking were over, she was all too aware of the spark that was still, clearly, between them.

Joel smiled and nodded; he paused, as if he was going to say something more, then eventually turned and walked away.

Good grief! Rosa stared at the door as he disappeared and closed it behind him. What a thing to share, with the history they had! Making wedding cakes — unbelievable.

20

'Where have you been?' Luke was pale and looked more like a man who was being led to the block than a man who was going to exchange his wedding vows in an hour or so. 'I seem to have forgotten the art of tying a cravat.'

'Is there an art to it?' Joel raised his eyebrows. He moved over to his friend and deftly tied the purple silk cravat. 'See? It's easy.'

'Thanks,' Luke said, grudgingly. 'So where were you?'

Joel grinned. 'Making cakes, as it happens.'

'Cakes?' Luke was astounded. 'It's my wedding day, you're supposed to be making sure I'm calm and chilled, and you piss off to make cakes?'

'Yes. I pissed off to make your wedding cakes. All fifty of them. Oh. Fifty-one. Rosa did a big one for you to cut.' He went into the bathroom which was still steamy from Luke's ablutions, and switched the shower on. Last night they had shared the room. Tonight, though, Luke and Erica would be in the bridal suite, and he would be back home in Robin Hood's Bay.

'Wedding cakes?' Luke rushed towards the bathroom and halted in the doorway. 'What the hell do you mean?'

'I mean,' said Joel, enjoying the situation possibly more than he should be, 'that Bridezilla crapped out and didn't order a cake. Now, if you'll excuse me, I need to get showered. I've got a wedding to attend. Off you go.' He waved his hand, gesturing for Luke to leave.

'She didn't order a cake?' Luke refused to budge.

'Is there an echo in here? Nope. She didn't order a cake.'

'And her mum didn't either?'

'Apparently not.'

'So you *made* fifty cakes?'

'Fifty-one. Just as well you booked a

hotel isn't it? With a kitchen and all that.'

'How the hell did you make fifty cakes?'

'Fifty-one. That echo's back. Look. I really, *really* don't want to get into this right now. I need to get ready. But trust me, your cake is covered.' Joel reached out and pushed the door closed, forcing Luke to step away. 'And if you let me get ready, I can make sure you get married.'

'Knock yourself out,' muttered Luke.

Joel locked the door and grinned as he began to strip off. His clothes and hair still smelled of cupcakes and baking, and he suspected Rosa's would too. He shook his head in pure admiration of her. She'd always been organised and practical, even in the short time they'd been together — but she'd always seemed to hold herself back, just a little bit. It was clear to him that she found her creative escape in baking, even though she was obviously extremely practical in the rest of her life.

Joel selected one of the little bottles of shower gel the hotel had kindly left in the bathroom and stepped into the shower cubicle. A paradox. That was what Rosa was.

It kind of suited her, in an odd way. He liked it.

21

Rosa had iced the cupcakes, and they were now decorated with creamy swirls in lavender and white icing. Some were studded with silver balls, some were dusted with rose petals and some had lavender heads balanced on top of the swirls.

The centrepiece was a buttercream-iced Victoria sponge with a bloom of summer petals on the top, trailing down the sides. Rosa carried the big cake carefully into the function room, and smiled at Ailsa who was already in there, arranging the fifty cupcakes on a tiered display.

'Rosa, this is incredible.' Ailsa tucked one of the cupcakes more securely into the display. 'I didn't even think it would be so simple to resolve.'

'Oh there's a lot of smoke and mirrors with these cupcakes.' Rosa placed the big cake on a glass serving dish and adjusted it so the trail of flowers was displayed to its best advantage. 'They're really simple; just vanilla fairy cakes with a hell of a lot of calories whirled on the top.'

'I bet they taste amazing. They certainly look it.'

'The 'look' is what it's all about today. They'll want some nice photos of themselves cutting the big cake, then everyone will just plough their way through the little ones, until there's nothing left but crumbs.'

'You cynical thing,' said Ailsa with a laugh. 'Wouldn't you want everything to look perfect if you were getting married?'

'I'm sure I would,' replied Rosa, tweaking a petal, 'but I don't know if I'd even bother to get married, to be honest. I could be happily unmarried. Happily co-habited. Happily coupled. Whatever the buzzwords are for it now. I've seen what a sniff of an engagement ring can do to someone, believe me.'

She shuddered, thinking of Iris and, latterly, the unholy wails that had come from the hotel room earlier. Honestly, was it even worth the stress?

'What about your sister? She seems happy enough.' Ailsa tugged the corner of the white tablecloth straighter and finally moved away from the display to retrieve her iPad.

'Jessie? She is. But it's different for her — they've got children. It means they've all got the same surname. She didn't do a big fussy thing. Mind you.' Rosa laughed, remembering. 'She was pregnant at the time so even the smell of the champagne toast turned her stomach. Bless her. Oh, and Elijah got tipsy as he decided to drink it for her. It was downed in one, before they could stop him.'

'You're laughing though, aren't you? So it must have been fun,' said Ailsa, hugging the iPad to her. Ailsa loved her job. She genuinely loved wedding planning. Rosa thought it would be an awful job.

'Oh it was definitely a fun wedding,' agreed Rosa. 'It was lovely — just at the church at Hartsford Hall, you know? The stately home in the village near to where they live? It's so pretty there. But no. Being a bridesmaid was enough for me, thanks.'

'And how did your other sister cope with wearing something other than black?'

'I will never know,' replied Rosa honestly. 'Angel wasn't too bad when she realised it was red, but she hated the style.' She shook her head. 'No. She wasn't impressed with something un-flouncy. I think the fact it was lace mollified her a bit though. And anyway, it was Jessie's day so — tough.' She grinned.

Jessie had looked gorgeous; her blonde hair had been loose and she had carried a small, round posy of white flowers. Her white lace dress skimmed her knees, set off by elbow length sleeves and a straight, slashed neck. A white, satin sash had been tied under her bust, her tummy just a little bit rounded; the first real evidence that Lottie had definitely been on her way. They'd arranged it all in a bit of a rush, had Jessie and Miles — but nobody seemed bothered and everybody smiled, all day. Well, apart from Angel who had grimaced at odd moments, when she plucked at her dress and thought nobody was watching. And their mother had sobbed tears of joy all day, and told everyone she couldn't be prouder of her girls. And didn't Angel just look *beautiful* in red? Such a nice change.

Rosa had created the wedding cake as well — a chocolate cake, topped and sandwiched with whipped cream, interspersed with strawberries, raspberries and cherries. A big red posy of poppies graced the top of the cake; Rosa had thought it might turn out to be rather vile, but as it was all that Jessie wanted, and indeed craved, she had to make it. It had actually turned out quite nice, to be fair.

'God, is that the time?' Ailsa interrupted Rosa's reverie as a clap and a cheer went up from the adjoining room. 'He must have kissed the bride.'

'Time for me to disappear, then,' said Rosa. 'It's all sorted in here now, so I'll skedaddle.'

'Thanks again for this,' said Ailsa. 'Erica really appreciates it, I know. She said she would be forever grateful and her mum said just to send the bill to her when you work out how much it was. It would have taken tons of sugar, I bet.'

'Loads of the stuff.' Rosa grimaced. 'I think I'm quite off buttercream at the minute. I've breathed too much icing sugar in and I can still taste it. Tell Mumzilla I'll have a word with catering and let her know the cost.'

'*Mumzilla?*' Ailsa shrieked with laughter. 'You're the second one to say that. She's a perfectly lovely lady.'

Rosa blushed to the roots of her hair. 'Oh. It was something Joel said the other day — ' She stopped talking. Ailsa would guess they hadn't just met today.

146

But what did it matter really?

'Joel? The other day? Nice.' She winked. 'He was the one who said it to me just before.'

'It's not like that. We knew each other years ago. We bumped into each other when he came to see what the hotel was like.'

'Ah,' said Ailsa, nodding. 'Nice.'

Rosa shook her head. 'If you say so. Okay, I'm skedaddling. I'm hiding from Chef if anyone's looking for me. There'll be no cakes made here for the rest of the day. I've wiped him out of ingredients. In fact — I may even be at the supermarket, stocking back up.'

'Okay!' Ailsa checked the clock again. 'Time for me to pop outside and supervise the photo shoot. See you later!'

'See you.' Rosa hurried out of the door. She took one last, lingering look at the display, smiled to herself, and rushed away down the corridor.

22

Joel was pleased he had been a considerable distance away from Erica when she screeched with joy at the sight of her hastily constructed wedding cake display; he might have been temporarily deafened. By the pained expression on Luke's face, it was more than likely the groom had suffered a similar fate.

'Oh my *God!*' Erica squealed, hanging on to Luke with one arm and waving the bouquet in the other hand towards the cakes. Joel wondered if she'd maybe been at the mini-bar before the ceremony; the woman seemed hyper. 'Look! *Look!*'

'Erica, I don't know if you're saying my name or ordering me to do something,' said Luke with an attempt at humour. His colour had returned, and he looked a lot more relaxed now. There had been a sticky moment when

Joel thought his best friend was going to slide, insensible, to the floor as he said his vows. He'd made it, though — and for better or worse, Luke and Erica were married.

'The cakes. Look at the *cakes*! Ailsa said it was sorted — she said it was done.'

Luke flashed a grateful smile at Joel; he knew who had helped make that happen. 'Yeah. You need to thank Joel for that one, Ricky.'

'Joel? *Our* Joel?' Erica spun around, her dress swishing across the polished wooden floorboards. 'You did this?' Again, she gestured with the bouquet.

Joel grinned and shrugged.

He toyed with the idea of taking more of the credit than he was entitled to, but then thought better of it. 'No. I did some of it. I helped mix stuff and I picked the flowers, but it was all Rosa's doing.'

'Rosa? Rosa on Reception?' asked Erica. 'The blonde girl? The really pretty one we saw when we came in?'

'That's her,' agreed Joel. 'Rosa and I

go back a few years. If there was ever anyone who could get you out of a cake-less fiasco, it would be her.'

'I'll have to thank her,' said Erica.

She began to pull Luke towards the doorway, seemingly forgetting she had to stand and form a receiving line for their guests; but Luke gently tugged her back towards him and tucked her arm into his. 'I agree, but not right now. Right now, you need to show people how beautiful you are, and I need to show everyone how honoured I am to be your husband.'

It was the perfect thing to say. Erica gave a gurgle of sheer pleasure and kissed her new husband. Joel grinned and went to take his place in the line. He'd tell Rosa later how much of a success it had been — once he managed to escape from the reception.

★   ★   ★

Joel's opportunity came around at about six o'clock. The dinner was eaten, the champagne fountain was gasping its last as it demanded refilling, and people were in varying states of post-wedding disorder, just relaxing and waiting for the next part of the day.

Erica was draped around Luke, swaying with him on the dance floor, as the daytime reception slid seamlessly into the evening one, and Joel took the chance to slip out of the room and head towards Reception.

He pulled up short as he saw an efficient-looking, mahogany-haired girl sitting there instead of the blonde girl he had expected.

The dark-haired girl looked up and smiled, thanks to some sort of recep-tionist's sixth sense. Her name badge told him she was called Tara.

Tara's smile widened as she saw his suit. 'You're part of the wedding party,' she stated. 'Is everything all right? Do you need anything in there?'

Joel ran his fingers through his hair and pushed it back off his face. He looked around and frowned. 'I was just looking for Rosa, to be honest. I wanted to thank her for the wedding cakes.'

'Oh aren't they amazing? I would have nipped along to have a peek, but it was too late when I got here for my shift. Ailsa managed to get a picture on her iPad though. They had me drooling.'

'So — you're on shift now?' asked Joel.

Tara nodded. 'Yep. I'm here until one in the morning. I'll probably see your guys heading back to their room after the party's over.'

'Hmm.' Joel looked back over his shoulder towards the function room. 'I guess it'll get messy later. Do you know where Rosa is, then?'

'Home I suspect. I took over from her at five.'

Joel's heart sank. 'Is she back here tomorrow?'

Tara shook her head. 'No. She's back in on Tuesday morning. One a.m. until nine. Which she doesn't like very much. Then she's on that for a few days, I think.'

Joel pulled a face. He didn't know where she lived, and now he wouldn't even be able to see her in person until — what? Next week, maybe? How was it even so difficult to find someone and thank them?

'Okay,' he said and nodded to Tara. 'Okay. Just let her know, well, thanks, I suppose. You'll probably see her before I will. I'm Joel. Tell her Joel says thanks.'

'All right,' replied Tara. 'I'll do that. Enjoy the rest of your day — Joel.'

'You too,' he said, smiling briefly at her.

He turned away with the intention of going back into the reception — then he thought of the walled garden he had been in before and the fresh air and the pretty grounds of Carrick Park.

No. He wouldn't go back in there just yet. He'd pop outside for a bit first. He smiled to himself, thinking of Erica and Luke. It wasn't like they were going to miss him very much. So he turned again to face a different direction, and walked determinedly out of the big double doors.

Joel walked around the perimeter of the hotel, hearing the music thumping out of the function room as the disco seemingly got going. It seemed so long ago that he had been gathering rose petals and lavender heads for Rosa, but in reality it hadn't been more than a few hours ago. The sun was still shining and the bees were buzzing — more lazily now, but it all added up to a perfect summer early evening. Far in the distance, a ribbon of sea shone, sparkling blue in the golden light, and he felt his heart lift.

He followed the same path he had taken earlier, inhaling the fresh air deeply, the scent of the roses tickling his nose. He didn't know if he'd ever be able to smell one again without being transported to the walled garden at Carrick Park on an August day. Despite enjoying the relative peace and quiet, he knew he needed to think things through. The meeting on Thursday had proved to him yet again how much he had actually liked Rosa, even after all of these years.

Joel rounded the corner and his heart leapt: she was there, sitting on a bench in the middle of the walled garden. Her shoes were kicked off and her bare feet were stretched out in front of her. She hadn't gone home after all. The summer evening had held her in its arms at Carrick Park, just as it was holding him.

Without even thinking about what he was going to say to her, he broke into a run and closed the distance between them.

23

Rosa had happily handed over the reception desk to Tara. She was wrecked — she hadn't baked anything on that scale for years; not since she'd worked in the industry.

The experience had brought back a lot of good memories, and she just wanted to go with the flow for a little while and enjoy the thoughts as they flooded into her mind. There was no better place than the walled garden, immersed in the scents of summer, to let them flood.

Just over the wall, she could see the moors rising in the distance then dropping away towards the coast. Some gulls were calling, swooping low and rising up on the air currents, going further and further out to sea. She was surrounded by the scent of freshly mown grass and full-blooming roses and lavender, and the little fountain in the centre of the garden trickled crystal-clear water into the pool below it. Carrick Park wasn't a bad place to work, really.

'Rosa!'

She twisted around. 'Joel!' Quickly, she stood up, forgetting she had no shoes on and wincing a little as a piece of gravel embedded itself into her sole. 'What are you doing out here?'

'I could ask you the same. I thought you'd gone home. Tara said . . . ' He flapped his hand in the direction of the room, obviously not needing to expand on that. 'But you didn't. I'm glad.'

'I was going to go home — but to be honest, I was having more fun spying in through the function room window and watching the wedding. Erica looks beautiful.' Rosa didn't elaborate on that fact that most of her attention had been on the best man, rather than the slightly sozzled bride. She'd hung around, probably more than was healthy, and knew it was really to catch fleeting glimpses of him.

'Did you see her? I think she's had a bit too much to drink. As has Luke and most of the other people in there.' He grinned. 'I'm the only one that's still sober. I'm driving home, so — ' He shrugged. 'Just a glass to toast them with, just to be polite.'

Rosa laughed. There was a very faint scent of champagne on his breath as he spoke, and she knew if they kissed that she would taste it too. She squished the idea down in case he read it in her face and looked behind her to make sure, as if the flowers were just too beautiful to turn one's back on.

'I made sure I picked ones that wouldn't show too much of a gap,' he admitted, apparently following her gaze. 'I got some funny looks off people.'

'You should have just mentioned my name if one of the gardeners had seen you.' She turned back to face him, half wondering why they were indulging in such small talk. 'Did you want me for anything in particular?' Pragmatic Rosa — always cutting to the chase.

'Just to — just to say thanks, really. The cakes have gone down well; one got nibbled by the page boy before they were served up, and the icing was licked off it, but everyone largely ignored that one.'

Rosa smiled. 'Kids make weddings, I think. Jessie's stepson kept us all amused at hers. I don't understand people who ban children from weddings. It makes no sense and it's just pretentious. They're family occasions. The whole family should be there.'

'Yep. He's Erica's godson. They didn't even consider it without him.'

And back to the small talk, thought Rosa with a private grimace. Iris had *really* done a number on him with regards to relationships. And the less said about her relationship with her ex, Jake, the better. Well, she had things to do and she couldn't spend all evening dancing around the subject of whether they should try again, or whether they shouldn't. 'So,' she said, 'enjoy the rest of the day, and I'll let you get back. If that's all it was.' She pasted another smile onto her face and turned to hunt for her shoes.

'Yes. Well. Thanks again,' replied Joel.

Rosa slipped her feet back into the high heels and picked up her bag from the seat. 'Goodbye, Joel. It was good to catch up with you. You know where I am if you need any cakes baking.' It was meant as a joke, and she hoped he would interpret it as such.

'I do indeed.' He was mock-serious. There was the briefest of pauses and then he reached out and pulled her towards him. Roughly, he kissed her and she was right; his lips tasted of champagne. They pulled away and his green eyes studied her for a moment. 'I know exactly where you are. Now.'

She dropped her head and nodded briefly. 'Yes. Okay. Bye then.' And she turned away from him and walked through the walled garden towards to the main drive of the hotel and the car park. She tilted her chin and held her head high in that defiant Tempest gesture. No need. Absolutely no need for him to see how rattled she actually was.

She held onto the hope that, after a moment or so, she would hear his footsteps running after her, and she even slowed down, just in case. But no. After a few more moments, just before she turned the corner, she turned and looked over her shoulder to see if he was watching her.

But he wasn't. He'd gone; disappeared somewhere like the ghosts that were supposed to haunt this place. But she knew he wasn't a ghost, as she could still taste the champagne from his kiss.

24

Rosa decided that she'd take a bit of a diversion home. She was too fizzy with excitement to go straight there, even though she was half-dead from tiredness. It wasn't a great combination.

Without giving herself much time to think about it, she took the turning towards Whitby, rather than the turning towards her village. Just on the outskirts of the town, amidst the old Victorian buildings and opposite Pannett Park, Rosa pulled into a spot outside one of the houses and turned off the engine.

She picked up her phone and sent a quick text: *Are you in? xxx*

Darling girl! Always for you! X came the response.

Rosa smiled. *I'm outside. Open up! X*

She looked up and the door to the house she was parked outside swung open. An elderly man stood in the doorway, another elderly man dotting around behind him, waving madly, a tea-towel clutched in his other hand.

Rosa jogged up the paved drive, waving equally madly. 'Donald! Anthony! How are you?'

'All the better for seeing you,' said Donald, at the front. Rosa hid a smile, noticing that they were in almost identical pullovers again, despite it being August. She wondered if they did it deliberately, or whether it was just part and parcel of being one half of a couple for more than forty years.

'I'm sorry for barging in,' she said, extricating herself from a hug that smelled of, and was just as comforting as, spiced fruit cake. 'But I just needed to see you. You know?'

'We know,' said Donald. He sniffed, suspiciously. 'Do I smell vanilla on you?'

'Vanilla and . . . sugar,' commented Anthony. 'You've been baking, haven't you?'

'I have! And so have you. Fruit cake, if I'm not mistaken.'

'Granny's best recipe, naturally,' agreed Anthony. 'What were you doing?'

'A last-minute wedding cake. Or should I say fifty-one last minute wedding cakes.'

'No!' The men chorused their horror and Rosa giggled.

'It's all right. Fifty of them were cupcakes. There was a mix-up and we had no cake for a wedding. I wanted to come and tell you — you know, so you could be proud of me.'

This time it was Anthony who hugged her. 'Always proud of you, darling.'

'I wish you'd taken over the bakery,' lamented Donald. 'I had hoped it, you know.'

Rosa blushed. 'I know. I'm sorry. It wasn't the right time.' She found herself urged forwards into the lounge. Nigel, the Westie dog, looked up and wagged his tail cheerfully as she walked in then bum-shuffled his way to the other side of the sofa to make room for her. It was odd, but for all Rosa liked order and smartness, she never minded sitting amongst Nigel-hairs in this lovely, warm, welcoming home. It reminded her, she knew, of her childhood home in Harrogate; and Donald and Anthony had been, in their own way, substitute parents when she had moved away from Harrogate and closer to Whitby. They'd been there during some of her darkest days, and helped her out of the self-inflicted mire she'd slipped into, after the Jake fiasco and the Joel fall-out.

'When *will* it be the right time for you to take the bakery on?' asked Donald. 'I still live in hope.'

'I don't know,' admitted Rosa. Anthony had bustled out to make her a cup of tea and, if she was lucky, he'd bring a slice of warm fruit cake in as well. 'Maybe when I've got children and don't think shift work agrees with me any more.' She laughed, mirthlessly.

'Yeah, that probably equates to never.'

'Now don't be like that!' scolded Donald. 'Don't write yourself off and please keep an open mind. We still own the bakery building, you know. It's your inheritance if you want it, we always said it was.' Donald sat down and Nigel jumped off the settee and ran over to him, clambering up onto his knee. 'Oh Nigel. You know you're not supposed to go on the furniture.' He stroked the dog in long, smooth motions from nose to tail and the little animal trembled with pleasure. 'You three were always our girls, you know,' admitted Donald. He blushed a little. 'We always loved you and we'll always be there for any one of you.'

'Oh yes. We only wanted what was best for you, Rosa. We still do. That Jake was bad news,' interjected Anthony. Rosa thrown a little at the comments was, nevertheless, delighted to see that there was indeed cake on the tray Anthony carried over, along with some chocolate biscuits. 'We never liked him.

Joel was much better — but you wouldn't be told, would you?' He slid the tray onto a coffee table.

'Well it might interest you to know that Joel helped me bake the cakes,' offered Rosa, feeling a small, disloyal stab of triumph as Anthony slopped the tea a little in the saucer whilst pouring it out and stared at her incredulously.

'Joel helped?' Donald leaned forwards and Nigel slid inelegantly off his knee.

'Yes. He turned up as best man for the cake-less wedding, and he asked me if I could suggest anything. I couldn't really do much else, but help out. Even though weddings don't agree with me.'

'I'm even more proud of you now,' said Donald, 'if that's even possible. Well done you.'

'Thank you.' Rosa ducked her head and took a sip of her tea. 'But what am I going to do about Joel?'

'Did he help you out very well with the fifty-one cakes?' asked Anthony.

'He was a star.' Rosa smiled.

'Then he's definitely a keeper,' stated Donald stoutly. 'If you can work with someone in the kitchen, you can absolutely build a relationship with them.'

'Do you think?' asked Rosa.

'I know,' responded Donald. 'Look at us. What other proof do you need?'

'Very true,' replied Rosa. 'Very true.'

25

Did you decide what to do about Joel?

It was three o'clock in the morning, a couple of days after her visit to Donald and Anthony, and Rosa was manning a very quiet reception desk. Her mobile phone was next to her, and a text had pinged through from Jessie.

Lottie misbehaving? Rosa typed, smiling at the idea. *As it happens, Joel made that decision for us. He thanked me for the cakes and I haven't heard from him since.*

Yes, the evil baby. You haven't heard from him? Honestly. Men!

Ha ha. Just because you got knocked up by a man, and seeing life at three in the morning is your reward, typed Rosa.

Ha bloody ha. Jessie had never enjoyed losing sleep. *What are you going to do?*

Nothing. Ships that pass in the night. Not wasting time over him, replied Rosa, more blithely than she felt, really. *Donald and Anthony think I should go for it but I'm not.*

Bless you. Okay. Here if you need me xxx In fact, I'll be here all night. Ha ha haaaaaa . . .

Rosa snorted out a laugh. She signed off with a 'love you' and went back to the computer. There was a message in the inbox that had just come in as well. What was it with this time in the morning? Why were people communicating? She sighed, thinking it was possibly an overseas enquiry from somewhere in a different time zone and opened it up.

It was from somewhere called CreativeComms and she rolled her eyes, thinking it was something spam-like.

Dear Sirs, it started. Rosa pulled a face. How generic. It was possibly marketing after all. *I was wondering whether you would be able to help me. I am in desperate need of a cake. Not just one cake, but maybe half a dozen. Maybe more. Maybe fifty-one. I will be in the area in the near future and do hope you can assist. Yours hopefully.*

There was no name on the end of the email and Rosa stared at the screen, her heart pounding. Her fingers hovered over the keyboard; it could be entirely genuine. It could be mean-spirited. It could even be a massive coincidence. Who the hell were these Creative-Comms people anyway?

She clicked on the internet browser and typed in the name of the company. At the top of the search results was a company based, it seemed, in Yorkshire. Rosa opened up their webpage and her eyes widened. Her heart flip-flopped around a little as she saw a very familiar face looking back at her. She would recognise those green eyes and that dark hair anywhere. *Joel Leicester; Advertising Executive; CreativeComms.*

Well, two could play at that game.

Almost without thinking, she clicked reply and began to type an email.

Dear Sirs, Thank you for your enquiry. This is a hotel; not a bakery. Many thanks.

She sat back and folded her arms. She didn't have to wait long.

Dear Sirs. A hotel? My goodness. And here was I thinking it was the best producer of botanical cakes in the county. But perhaps you misunderstand me. I am desperate for a cake. I will stop at nothing.

Rosa's mouth twitched, a smile threatening to break through. Her fingers flew across the keyboard.

Dear Sirs. I believe you misunderstand me. This is a hotel and we do not produce cakes at will for strangers in the early hours of the morning. We bid you a goodnight.

It only took a few seconds for the next response to come in.

Ah Rosa. Please?

Her eyes widened.

No Joel.

172

She leaned forward and stared at the screen, willing him to respond.

Instead, a cool night breeze enveloped her as the door opened and a shadow fell across her:

'Rosa. I mean it. Please? Look — I even brought the tea.'

She jerked her head upwards and he was standing there, a silver flask in his hand, two plastic mugs dangling from his fingertips. He looked unshaven but quite awake, considering it was stupid o'clock in the morning. His eyes were glinting emerald fire, his hair darker than the night outside. Rosa caught her breath.

'Where on earth were you?' She stood up, the chair shooting away behind her on its wheels.

'In the car park,' admitted Joel. He shrugged. 'I was thinking.' He put the cups and the flask on the reception desk and grinned at her. His smile lit the foyer. It was unfair that he was so gorgeous, it really was.

'*Thinking?*' Rosa asked, still staring

at him. 'Sitting in the car park *thinking*?'

He cupped his hand against his ear and stared off into the distance. 'That echo's back. How odd.' He moved his hand. 'Yes. I couldn't sleep, so I went for a drive. It's a beautiful evening. I just followed the road — I wasn't even sure where I was going. But,' he shrugged again, 'my subconscious seemed to know where I was going. So I ended up here.'

'Less of the flannel,' said practical Rosa, her face stony. 'If that was even remotely true, you wouldn't have had the flask prepared would you?'

Joel had the grace to look sheepish. 'Okay. You got me. Will I never be able to surprise you with a grand romantic gesture?'

Rosa sighed. 'A grand romantic gesture? Did we even manage one of those when we were together? Beyond Cornwall, that is.'

'Quite possibly not,' admitted Joel. 'But we *did* go to Cornwall. That should count.'

'It did. But it was kind of ruined by the fact that you had a sitting tenant when we got back.'

'You didn't even let me explain, though. If you'd listened, then you'd know she was just chancing her luck. She'd let herself in. She was never invited there. She shouldn't even have *been* there. We weren't together. You didn't give me the chance to tell you anything about it.'

'What was I *supposed* to think?' Rosa folded her arms defensively. 'She was sitting there, in her horrid satin pyjamas reading a wedding magazine.'

'She'd kept her copy of the key. I changed the locks the next day, just in case she had another one stashed somewhere. I tried to tell you all that. I tried every bloody *way* to tell you that.' He paused and scratched his head. Rosa's eyes unwittingly travelled upwards to see the mess he'd made of his hair. She longed to reach out and smooth it down for him but clenched her fists instead. 'It's a shame you didn't make it easier for me,' he continued. 'We've missed out on a good few years, haven't we?'

'But I didn't want to stay with you. I wanted to get away from you. You hurt me.'

Joel frowned. 'But it was honestly over with Iris, even when you saw her. Very much over. Yes, we had been engaged. Yes, we were planning a wedding — but that was months before I met you. You have to believe me. I tried so hard to find you. I went to the bakery, and they said you were taking the week off and they were closing. I went back a few weeks later and asked the florist next door where you'd gone and she said she didn't know. And I went to your flat and this weird woman opened the door and said you'd moved. I went to Staithes and was pretty certain I'd found your sister in her bookshop, but that didn't really help. And amongst all that, I tried to call you and found out you'd changed your number. Then I tried to send you some messages on Facebook.' He grimaced. 'But I think you blocked me.'

'I did block you. I was so angry with you.'

'Well that proves it. I couldn't contact you, and you'd made it rather clear that you didn't even *want* me to contact you. So next thing I know, it's six years later and I walk into the hotel where my friend is getting married — and there you are. You and your baking skills. And it's like those six years never happened.'

'But you can't just expect to pick up after all that time and for it all to be the same; for *us* to be the same,' said Rosa. 'You know, you've never even asked me if I've got anyone else in my life. You're just coming in here and lying to me about random moonlit drives — yes, it's a lie, don't try to deny it — and then building up to . . . *something* . . . which I haven't quite worked out yet.'

'*Do* you have anyone?'

'No.'

'There you go. I've asked you now and you haven't. Any more complaints?'

'Joel . . . do *you*? Do you have anyone else.' She half-dreaded the answer.

'No. Absolutely not.'

'Oh.'

He raised his eyebrows and remained silent. It was clearly her turn to speak.

'Good grief. You can't just interrupt my work.' Rosa tried a different tack. 'I'm very busy.'

'You look it.' Joel stared around the empty foyer. 'As always. As you apparently are every time I pop up and surprise you.'

'I have to be on call in case anyone wants anything,' she said thinly. 'I don't have time for chit-chat — with you, or with anyone else. You should probably go.'

'Fair comment. Would you be able to have a cup of tea, though? Before I go. Just here, just in the hallway, just on those nice seats over there.' He pointed to the area where the Carrick Park books had been recently restocked and the inviting squashy seats and low tables.

'I could probably stretch to a cup of tea,' Rosa said with a sigh. 'But I don't want to go over there. Let's go to the doorway. I wouldn't mind some fresh air, to be honest. You've rattled me. I'll have to admit that to my sisters now and they'll laugh and laugh.'

Joel grinned. 'There's more I could do than just rattle you,' he said, lowering his voice enticingly.

Rosa rolled her eyes and stepped out from behind the desk. 'I'm at work,' she said. 'Let's just have a cup of tea for now.'

'For now?' Joel jumped on the phrase and smiled one of his rare, wicked smiles.

'Yes,' said Rosa shortly, refusing to be led. She walked to the big heavy doorway and stepped just outside, dropping the doorstopper in place and propping it open. From here she could hear the phone and see if anyone wandered to the desk for anything. She could also take a deep breath of the cool night air and close her eyes, catching the familiar, salty tang in the scent of the breeze. It gave her enough time to collect herself, anyway, whilst Joel unscrewed the flask and poured two mugs of hot, steaming tea.

'It's a shame we have no cake to go with it,' he said. Rosa didn't deign to respond. Joel laughed quietly and shook his head, handing one of the plastic mugs to her. 'It was a pretty good recovery, wasn't it? Luke's wedding.'

'It seems like a lifetime ago.' She leaned against the doorframe and looked out along the sweeping gravel drive where the little lamps flickered in two neat lines, guiding visitors to the Park. 'But there's no more perfect place to get married than Carrick Park. I suspect having no cake wouldn't have entirely ruined *everything*.'

'You have no idea.' Joel leaned on the other side of the frame and followed her gaze along the driveway. 'Erica wouldn't have seen it like that. It's nice here, isn't it, though? Do you ever wonder what the people were like who owned it? Ever worry that they'll appear when you're on night shift and go 'Boo!' I read that book, you know. The one I picked up for you, when you dropped it, before the wedding; Butter-fingers.'

Despite herself, Rosa laughed and turned to face him. 'I worry about the ghosts no more than I worry about strange men emailing me in the middle of the night from the car park. I don't think I've got anything to fear from the previous residents if they do appear. But I'm cynical. I don't believe it's haunted. Even though Lady Eleanor is supposed to play random stuff on the piano, and someone is supposed to have fallen down the stairs behind us there and been killed.' She nodded in the direction of the main stairs, where the famous Land-seer portrait of Lady Eleanor hung.

'But you'll know that if you've read the book, so I'll shut up now.'

"*All houses wherein men have lived and died are haunted houses. Through the open doors the harmless phantoms on their errands glide, with feet that make no sound upon the floors*," quoted Joel, his voice little more than a whisper. He sipped his tea, his eyes burning into hers, and Rosa shivered.

'It's that Longfellow poem. I know. You're a show-off. And I still don't believe it.'

'Should I come again at Whitby Goth Weekend and try again? Recite it at Halloween, perhaps?'

'No, there's no need for that,' said Rosa briskly. 'Angel's got me immune to that sort of carry on, thanks very much. Most of it's in her mind. I tell you, she kept saying her house was haunted for years and then decided she didn't like the idea of ghosts very much after all.'

'So you're still the practical one.' Joel looked at her, expecting, she realised, the chit-chat to continue. Rosa bit her lip, annoyed at the fact he'd managed to engage her in conversation when she was supposed to be angry at him for turning back up at the hotel.

'You're presumptuous.' She turned away again, looking at the flickering lights.

'I might be presumptuous, but tell me I've got reason to hope, at least?' She was aware that he had taken a step towards her. There was a tiny click as he put the mug down on the cool, worn, stone step. She felt a gentle pressure on her arm as he took hold of it and turned her to face him. The scent of roses wrapped itself around her, brought to her on a summer breeze. It reminded her of his presence in the kitchen; his dizzying presence and the spark she knew was still there if only she admitted it . . .

Her heart began beating far too fast and she opened her mouth to protest, but he took the mug from her and placed it by his. Then he stood up and pulled her close. He was exactly as she had remembered him; it was exactly how it should be.

They had shared a kiss or two that day, the day she had baked the wedding cakes, but it had been nothing like this; nothing as slow and as considered as this. She was aware of a hundred things she had dismissed before: the way the light shone through a moth's wing as it skittered into the floodlights; the whisper of a breeze as it lifted a loose strand of hair from the nape of her neck; the warmth of his touch on her cool skin; the dizzying fall into blackness if she looked away over the moors, away from the floodlit safety of Carrick Park . . . everything just distilled in that one moment of awareness, distilled into his presence, his heat, his scent —

'Joel,' she murmured, her lips seeking his. 'What are we doing?' For a split second, she was the moth at Carrick Park, the moth in Cornwall, flying destructively towards its fate.

'What we should have done before,'

he murmured back. He nuzzled into her and nipped her bottom lip gently between his teeth. She felt her knees buckle, remembering how she had always fitted into his arms, how he was the only one who had ever had this effect on her.

'I had to walk away,' she whispered. 'I had to. I wasn't going to stay with someone who had a fiancée.'

'But she wasn't my fiancée any more,' he persisted. 'I wish you'd waited to find out the truth.'

'I couldn't. Joel, I never told you this — but I was married. He cheated on me. I wasn't going to put up with it again.'

She felt Joel stiffen. There now. That had thrown him.

26

Jake had definitely been a mistake. A huge mistake. It had lasted all of six months — a Las Vegas wedding on holiday, celebrating the end of university and two years together as boyfriend and girlfriend. It had seemed a good idea at the time, even though her parents and her uncles had despaired of her and, quite rightly, predicted that it wouldn't end well.

She never talked about Jake and she was pretty sure he would never talk about her either. It had, in short, been something she wished she could sweep under the carpet and forget about.

The reason she'd banned her sisters from ever mentioning him, was the fact that it was all actually rather humiliating. She was Rosa. She was supposed to be the sensible one. She'd come back from Las Vegas, packed her bags and moved into an awful studio flat above an off-licence. She and Jake had got jobs at a wine bar, confident they could start at the bottom and work their way up.

The flat had, in fact, been an extension of their student lifestyle — parties every weekend, all weekend, and friends dropping by at all hours.

Nineteen-year-old Angel had been one of her most frequent visitors — Angel and her some-time boyfriend/sometime-friend Zac. It had been in Rosa's flat that Angel and Zac had got too drunk one evening to see sense and decided it would be a good idea to sleep together.

It had been in Rosa's flat that twenty-year-old Jessie had tried tequila for the first and last time — it had been Rosa who had held her sister's honey-coloured hair back from her face as she threw up in the toilet.

'I'm going to *die* and Mum and Dad will just *kill* me if I do!' Jess had howled. Jake had, helpfully, a large glass of wine ready for Jessie when she finally stumbled out of the toilet; which was, Rosa realised, as she squinted through a haze of cigarette smoke, probably not the best thing for Jessie under the circumstances. Jessie had thought differently; she'd drained the lot and passed out on the sofa. But it was all okay because one of their fellow guests was a medical student and he said she was completely fine.

Rosa had got the job at the bakery when she realised the rent wouldn't pay itself and their bar jobs didn't really cut it. She was lucky that Donald and Anthony owned the place and were able to take her on, and were there to mop up her tears when Jake had, eventually, thought it would be a good idea to bring a girl from the wine bar home, when Rosa was out perfecting cream slices.

It wasn't the first time he'd been unfaithful, but it was the first time he'd literally been caught in the act. Later, Rosa had thought how ironic it was that it had taken longer to get divorced than it had taken to get married.

So no: weddings weren't the best of things for Rosa, and she had hated the whole idea for a long, long time.

'I think you're jealous that you didn't have a proper wedding,' Angel had whispered to her as the sisters were lined up in a pew, guests at their cousin's wedding, a few years later. Their parents flanked them, either side and Rosa knew Angel was whispering so her mother didn't scold her. She'd often been told off for starting arguments and this, it seemed, was no exception.

Rosa had stiffened and sat up straight. 'It was a proper wedding,' she had said, defending herself. 'It just wasn't a proper marriage.'

'It was *not* a proper wedding,' Angel had hissed. She'd pointed a back-tipped nail at Rosa and wagged her finger. 'We weren't there. We weren't bridesmaids.'

Rosa looked at the littlest bridesmaid toddling unsteadily down the aisle — it was the bride's niece and she was all of eighteen months old. Rosa flinched as the child face-planted the floor then scrambled to her feet and continued to waddle towards her aunt.

'Bridesmaids,' she said dismissively. 'You weren't so bothered about that when you used to come to the flat.'

'The flat was the best part of that fiasco,' muttered Angel.

'Which flat?' Jessie leaned in, afraid she was missing out on anything.

'Girls!' Their father hissed. 'Watch the wedding, will you?'

They'd been silent long enough to watch the bridesmaid wipe her nose on the bride's train.

Then Angel had continued. 'Rosa's flat. The one she had with Jake,' she supplied helpfully.

'Oh! *That* flat!' Jessie nodded thoughtfully. 'Dodgy area, though.'

'Very dodgy,' agreed Angel. She flashed a sly look at her sister. 'Alcoholic beverages and stuff — rife. All rife.'

'Just shut up!' hissed Rosa, clenching her handbag tightly for fear of lashing out at either or both of her sisters. 'It was a mistake, all right? We're all entitled to make mistakes and at least I got out of it.'

'*Girls!*' Their mother could be the fiercest Tempest of all, and they eventually shut up to watch the rest of the wedding.

But Rosa had indeed got out of it. She'd kept her job and got herself a nicer flat, over the deli-café instead; which smelled a whole lot better when she came down in a morning. And the rest, as they say, was history. Rosa had worked her way up through the ranks at the bakery, studied alongside Donald and Anthony, and perfected her baking. She'd worked in hospitality, done reception work and now she was at Carrick Park in a job she loved and owned a house that was possibly tiny and buttoned-up, but it was in a nice village and there wasn't a student party in sight.

No wonder she was more than cynical about weddings, and more than sensitive about dating men with fiancées —

'You were married?' Joel's soft voice cut through the uncomfortable memories.

'Yes,' Rosa replied, stiffly. 'He was called Jake. We were twenty-one. It lasted six months. That's about all you need to know.' She tried to pull away, but to her surprise he tightened his grip on her and pulled her more closely towards him.

He leaned down and bent his head more closely to her neck. He kissed her gently enough and expertly enough to make her already wobbly legs even more unsteady. She closed her eyes and arched her body instinctively towards him, catching her breath and raising her face to the heavens.

'Well. So you were married.' He punctuated his words with another kiss. 'And I had a fiancée who was no longer a fiancée.' He kissed her again. 'And you had a husband who's no longer a husband. So I think that makes us even. Don't you?'

'Joel . . . ' She tried to pull away but found that she didn't really want to after all. So she allowed him to kiss her some more and prayed that no customers would telephone her, and certainly that nobody would come to the desk.

27

Having her in his arms was like being back in Cornwall all over again. His sensory memory was sparking into life, as if it had been dead and buried for the last six years.

In fact, what had he to show for the last six years? Yes, he had thrown himself into his career, made a success of it, ditched the beaten-up VW and bought his Audi. He'd traded the flat in for a house, and he'd had several girlfriends, the sum total of those relationships not even lasting as long as Rosa's marriage. But that was it. He was missing something, had been missing something for all that time. And now it made sense. There was and always had been a vanilla-and-sugar scented Rosa-shaped hole in his top-show perfect life.

Now there were no cakes, no bowls

of buttercream and no Bridezillas — in whatever incarnation they took — between them at all. There was just him and her, Joel and Rosa, and nothing else in the world.

'What time do you finish,' he whispered. 'What time is your shift over?'

'Nine o'clock. Five hours.'

'I don't have time to go home, then,' he said. He could feel her smile against his chest.

'Yes you do. I know where you live.'

'How do you know that?'

'Something clever called the bookings system.'

'So you looked me up?' He was amused.

'Not at all. I wanted to know who I should charge the cupcakes to if they refused to pay up and said they were rubbish.'

'You're the only one that's talking rubbish.' He kissed her again and drew away reluctantly. 'I don't want you to, but you should probably get back to work.'

'Probably.'

'And what were you planning to do after work?'

'Go home. Chill for a bit. Eat. And sleep.' She pulled away with a sigh. 'I have an exciting life. Not quite within the remit of CreativeComms, but you know. It suits me.'

'Okay.' Joel nodded. 'I can work with that. I'll see you about nine-thirty, yes?'

'Nine-thirty?' Rosa stared up at him. 'What do you mean?'

'I mean exactly what I say. You have my address. I'll see you around about nine-thirty. It only takes about fifteen minutes normally, but you'll hit rush hour I suspect. I'll have your breakfast ready. So don't worry about anything, okay? You can eat, chill and sleep at my place. If you want?'

Rosa giggled, an unusual, girly sound that made Joel grin. He'd never really heard that giggle much, even in the time they'd spent together.

'I want,' she responded. 'Why the hell not?'

'Excellent.' He kissed her again and looked into her eyes. 'Maybe we should try again — just see how it goes?'

He could read the conflicting emotions in her face; he waited and was rewarded eventually with a nod.

'Perhaps. At least I have no husband. And you have no girlfriend.' She raised her eyebrows. 'If you're absolutely *sure* about that one?'

Joel laughed and shook his head. 'No. No girlfriend. No wife. And no fiancée. Thank God.'

Rosa smiled. 'Great. I'll see you at nine-thirty then.'

'See you at nine-thirty,' he said; and, unwillingly, released her.

★　★　★

Rosa kept the front door open, even when she was back at the reception desk. She saw the world outside begin to lighten, and finally wandered through the silent hotel to the old morning room and watched the sun rise, staining the sky a rosy pink.

Tara was due to relieve her at nine and by the time she arrived, the day had a promise of late summer in the air; it was already warm and sunny, the sort of morning that puts almost anybody into good spirits.

'Morning!' Rosa greeted Tara. 'It's been a quiet night. Nothing to report. No mess-ups with room service and nobody moaning that there's a spider in their bath.'

Tara laughed. 'The spider call wouldn't be the first one, would it?'

Rosa shook her head. 'Nope. Although I'd much rather have the spider to deal with than a seagull fly into the foyer again.'

'Ugh.' Tara shuddered. 'I remember it all too well. Anyway, have a good day. You heading upstairs for a little while or going home?'

Rosa couldn't hide her smile. 'Neither. I'm going to a friend's for breakfast.'

'Oh?' Tara raised her eyebrows.

'Anything I need to know about this friend?'

'Nothing.' Rosa grinned. 'He invited me last night, when we had a tea break together.'

'What?' Tara was immediately alert. 'A tea break? With company? On the night shift? I thought you said it had been quiet?'

'It *was* quiet. That's how I had time for a tea break. And no, I'm not telling you anything else. Forget it.' She stood and stretched, then moved to give Tara space behind the desk. 'See you!'

'See you!' said Tara. 'Have fun. I look forward to hearing about it. Oh! Was it the guy from the wedding who was looking for you? That really, really sexy one? God! I would have done him without a second thought — '

'Enough!' warned Rosa. 'Oh. And have fun today.' She scurried off before Tara had a chance to probe any deeper.

She slung her bag over her shoulder and caught up her jacket, hurrying out to the car. Once she was in it, she pulled out her ponytail band and brushed her fair hair through with her fingers until it hung about her shoulders looking far less severe than it had done last night. Finally, she toed off her high heels and slipped on her comfy driving shoes. She was as ready as she'd ever be.

28

Joel had been right. It took Rosa about twenty-five minutes to get to his house. It was in the new part of the town, as she had suspected, and a silver Audi stood on the driveway, glinting in the morning light.

Rosa pulled up in front of the house and stared at it for a few moments. She could see a movement in the window, as if someone had been sitting there, waiting for a visitor, then jumped to their feet. She smiled and switched off the engine just as the door opened.

He stood there, dark-haired, dishevelled, slightly embarrassed; just perfectly the Joel she had loved so briefly yet so strongly. He raised a hand and waved, and she waved back. She toyed with the idea of putting on the high heels again but thought her flatties were as good as anything. Then she took a deep breath and opened the car door.

He greeted her with a kiss, then stood to one side as she walked past him into the small, modern house.

'Straight through,' he said. 'Into the kitchen. I made breakfast, just as I promised. I remembered how you liked a fry-up. It's just keeping warm for you.'

The scent of bacon and sausages was hanging in the air and it made her mouth water. 'Nothing better to come back to,' she said with a grin. 'Thanks for this.'

'No problem. There's proper coffee as well for you. And, once you've finished that, there's one more thing that I think you'll like. I'll just go and start it off, then I'll come and join you, if that's okay?'

Rosa turned to him with a smile. 'Why wouldn't it be okay? I've been looking forward to this since four o'clock this morning.'

'Excellent. Here. Sit down. I'll be

back in a moment, I promise.'

She did as she was bid, and he disappeared upstairs. Rosa looked around at the little kitchen, clearly showing the signs that someone had been preparing a hearty breakfast, judging by the frying pan soaking in the sink and the faint haze of coffee-scented steam coming off the percolator in the corner.

She could get used to this — it was exactly as she'd imagined when she was asking her sisters for their opinions on Joel. Then her attention was caught by a noise upstairs — it sounded awfully like running water.

Joel's footsteps came hurrying down the stairs and he came into the kitchen. 'Okay. Now — brown sauce or red?'

'You're spoiling me!'

'I'm trying to make up for lost time. We agreed that we never had any great romantic gestures apart from Cornwall. Well — treating you to breakfast might not count as a great gesture either, but I think you deserve something special

203

after a hard night at work. I could have taken you out to a café, and I might just do that another morning. But today was special. Today, I wanted to prove that we can at least try to pick up where we left off and not have any exes in the picture.'

'No exes is good,' agreed Rosa.

'Great. Now — eat up, and then I have to insist you go upstairs and take your clothes off.'

Rosa almost choked on a bit of fried bread. 'Excuse me?'

'You'll see,' he said, with a wink.

A sweet scent was wafting down the stairs, overlaying that of the delicious breakfast. Rosa sniffed, turning her face to the door.

Then it struck her: 'Roses?' she asked. She turned back to Joel. 'Is that roses I can smell?'

Joel nodded. He blushed and reached out, placing his hand over hers. 'Roses for you, Rosa. I have to learn these grand gestures. I'm not very good at them. But I remembered you told me that most girls would go for rose petals to scatter into their bath. I've got rose bath salts in there, rose petals and a rose candle.' He flushed again. 'Too much?'

Rosa laughed and shook her head. She leaned over and kissed him. 'Not too much at all. Thank you. There's just one thing.' She smiled and bit her lip, hardly daring to believe that this was happening. 'I'm on this shift for the next four days. Which day can we go to the café?'

'Any day you like,' Joel replied, laughing. 'I can always pull the working from home card — CreativeComms is very flexible with the execs, you know. Because I also have a stash of lavender bath products, lily bath products, champagne and assorted chocolates. They've got to be used up somehow. Twenty-four hour supermarkets are wonderful things.'

Rosa nodded sagely. 'I think you're on track with the romantic gesture thing, but I'll need to train you up just a little bit more. Can you bear it?'

'I think I can. 'And any help you need with cakes, I'm your man. I think we could make a pretty good team. Can we forget the past and start again properly?'

'I think we could. I definitely think we could. But — ' she touched his hand gently ' — I don't want to forget Cornwall. I never want to forget Cornwall.'

'Me neither,' he agreed. 'And look. I kept this for you, all this time. Just in case I saw you again.' He turned and took a sea-green paper bag off the bench in the kitchen, patterned with cream polka dots. 'I'm sorry it's not your original copy — but I'm ninety nine point nine per cent sure I got it from your sister.' He grinned and handed the package over to her.

'What is it?'

'Open it and see.'

Rosa did as he suggested and peered inside it. 'Oh my. Oh my goodness. Joel!' She raised her face and stared at him. '*Green Smoke*. My book!'

'Not quite your book, like I say — but as close as, damn it.'

Rosa's hand shook as she took the precious item out of the bag. A small piece of paper fluttered onto the table and she picked it up and looked at it closely. 'The receipt,' she whispered, 'from Jessie's shop.' She smiled. 'And dated a week after our trip to Cornwall. Thank you.' She looked at him. 'This means so much. I'm sorry I was so awful. I'm sorry I got my sisters and my uncles to get between us. That was hideous behaviour — but after Jake, I'd lost all faith in everyone. I never thought I could be happy or trust someone again; so I buttoned myself up and built barriers and I was vile to you. I never let anyone close to me after that at all. I'm sorry I wasted all those years and didn't give you a second chance. And I'm sorry we never went to Cornwall again.'

'Perhaps we *could* go back, though? We could go and make some new memories. If you wanted to,' Joel suggested quietly. 'I once had a wonderful Dragon Day with a beautiful girl in Cornwall. I'd like another one, if possible.'

'Perhaps we could do that. And I think I *do* want to do that — very much.'

It was a delicious prospect.

Epilogue

Twenty perfectly proportioned cupcakes were lined up on a tray; ten had pink fondant icing bunny faces on them, and ten had pink fondant teddy faces. Twenty more cupcakes were lined up next to them; just plain, naked, golden sponge, waiting for the same treatment.

'I don't know what's worse,' commented Joel. 'Fondant icing or buttercream. It just all gets messy.'

'It gets messy if you mess with it too much,' said Rosa. 'You need to roll that out a bit thinner; then make sure your cutter is clean, as it'll cut sharper. I promise.'

'The teddies look startled,' mumbled Joel, placing a circle of icing on top of the basic teddy-face shape to make a muzzle.

'It's because you've made their

mouths too round,' said Rosa, glancing across. 'They're going 'oooooh'.'

'Ooooh,' repeated Joel, frowning. Then they looked at each other and collapsed into laughter.

'God, I hope your sister appreciates this,' he said. 'My fingers are like bloody sausages today.'

'She will,' promised Rosa. 'But by the time Lottie stuffs them in her mouth, it won't matter anyway.'

'Does Jessie really need forty cup-cakes and a massive fairy castle cake, for a two-year old's birthday party?' asked Joel, standing up and surveying the counter.

'Yes. She's very kindly invited half of Yorkshire to descend on our house. Said she was being extremely thought-ful, so I didn't have to transport everything to *her* house. But I mean, even putting Angel and Kyle *near* cake is inviting destruction. Then if Elijah decides to have some . . . ' She shrugged. Joel nodded. He knew what the boy was like.

'Then there's all the grandparents,' continued Rosa. 'And Donald and Anthony — Heaven help us if the cakes aren't right if *they're* here. Nigel will probably sneak some too, although he's not supposed to. And there's you, of course.' She stretched and pressed her hand into the small of her back. 'But I never thought *I'd* go off cake. Ever.'

Joel smiled as he looked at her. He walked over and laid a sticky, icing-covered hand on her neatly rounded tummy, the pale blue apron pulled tight over her burgeoning figure. 'Cornwall has a lot to answer for,' he said.

'A hell of a lot.' Rosa smiled and covered his hand with hers, pressing down gently. Beneath them, a firm, strong little foot pushed back.

'Any regrets?' he asked.

'Just the fact I've made all these cakes and I won't be enjoying any of them,' she said, 'but apart from that. No. None at all.'

'I'm glad to hear that.' He lifted a strand of hair from her cheek and tucked it behind her ear; a gesture so sweet and now so utterly Joel that Rosa felt a warmth creep over her that had nothing to do with the summer sunshine or the fact they were standing together in their nice, big, airy kitchen, next to an island that was perfect for setting cakes out on as she waited for them to cool, the scent of roses and lavender drifting in through the open window.

It was more that she was perfectly ensconced in the warmth you feel when you realise you've finally come home; you're finally where you should be. And no matter what has gone before, you know it's never going to be any better than the moment you're in, right here and right now.

Thank You

Thank you so much for reading, and hopefully enjoying, this novella — affectionately known by me as 'Rosa's Story'. I hope you enjoyed meeting the Tempest sisters and revisiting somewhere that is very close to my heart in the beautiful, if fictional, Carrick Park. And in case you were wondering, *Green Smoke* is a real book as well — one of my favourite books from childhood.

Dragon Days are the best days!

Authors need to know they are doing the right thing though, and keeping our readers happy is a huge part of the job. So it would be wonderful if you could find a moment just to write a quick review on Amazon or one of the other websites to let me know that you enjoyed the book. Thank you again, and do feel free to contact me at any time on Facebook, Twitter, through my

website or through my lovely publishers
Choc Lit.
Thanks again and much love to you
all,

Kirsty
xx

We do hope that you have enjoyed reading this large print book.

Did you know that all of our titles are available for purchase?

We publish a wide range of high quality large print books including:
**Romances, Mysteries, Classics
General Fiction
Non Fiction and Westerns**

Special interest titles available in large print are:
**The Little Oxford Dictionary
Music Book, Song Book
Hymn Book, Service Book**

Also available from us courtesy of Oxford University Press:
**Young Readers' Dictionary
(large print edition)
Young Readers' Thesaurus
(large print edition)**

For further information or a free brochure, please contact us at:
**Ulverscroft Large Print Books Ltd.,
The Green, Bradgate Road, Anstey,
Leicester, LE7 7FU, England.
Tel:** (00 44) **0116 236 4325
Fax:** (00 44) **0116 234 0205**

THE SIGNET RING

Anne Holman

Resigned to spinsterhood, Amy Gibbon is astounded to receive a proposal of marriage from Viscount Charles Chard upon their very first meeting! Love quickly flares in her heart, but Charles is more reticent — he needs an heir, and this is a marriage of convenience. Determined to win her new husband over, Amy follows him to the Continent, the dangers of the Napoleonic wars, where he must search for his father's precious signet ring which was stolen at Waterloo. Can true love blossom under such circumstances?

THE LOST YEARS

Irena Nieslony

Upon returning from their honeymoon in Tanzania, Eve Masters and her new husband David are quickly embroiled in chaos. When a hit-and-run accident almost kills them both, David develops amnesia and has no recollection of who Eve is. And then she pays a visit to his first wife — to find her dead body slumped over the kitchen table, with herself as the prime murder suspect! Will Eve be able to solve this tangled web, and will David remember her again — or will the villains win for the first time?